BELONGING TO HIM

OLIVIA ASHERS

Copyright © 2021 by Olivia Ashers

All rights reserved.

No part of this book may be reproduced in any form or by any electronic or mechanical means, including information storage and retrieval systems, without written permission from the author.

This is a work of fiction. Names, characters, places, and incidents either are products of the author's imagination or are used fictitiously. Any resemblance to actual events or locales or persons, living or dead, is entirely coincidental.

https://oliviaashers.com/

CHAPTER 1

Natalia

"HEY, NAT!" MY SISTER shouted from across the room. "What do you think about this one?"

I turned my head in her direction, narrowing my eyes at the pink cocktail dress she was holding in her hands.

A smile spread across her lips as she lifted the dress

up even more, closer to her face, her hazel eyes expectant.

"Um, I don't know," I said. "Isn't it a bit too open? The cleavage part, I mean."

Her brow furrowed as she looked down at the dress and then lifted her gaze to me again. "But that's the whole point. I think Enrico would like it."

I opened my mouth to ask if *she* liked it, or if she was only worried about what her husband would like, but I decided not to say anything.

Adelina was two years older than me, and she'd married Enrico Pagani four years ago. When I'd found out my dad agreed to marry my sister off to Enrico, who was thirteen years older than her, I'd been bawling my eyes out for days because I couldn't imagine my life without her.

We'd always done everything together, and we'd been inseparable. Now, I was lucky if I got to see her for a few hours when her husband allowed her to go shopping with me.

Today was one of those lucky days, and I so didn't want to get into a pointless fight with her, especially not about something as insignificant as a dress.

Adelina and I might be super close, but we still had our differences.

Plenty of them.

She always knew how to do and say the right thing, and I...

"Adelina, it's beautiful!" my mom said, taking hold of the dress. "You have to get this one."

"I know." Adelina grinned.

I sighed.

My mom and Adelina looked so much alike—it wasn't just because they both had long light brown hair they preferred to wear up—and they also liked the same things.

Or, well, they knew exactly what their husbands would like and how to make them happy, and in a way, that made them happy too.

I had no idea if I'd ever learn how to do that, or if I'd ever find myself in the role of a mafia princess and someone's wife.

A part of me secretly hoped I'd meet someone and fall in love, and we'd live happily ever after.

If my mom or Adelina could hear my thoughts right now, I was sure they'd be rolling their eyes.

My mom would say I should be grateful for all the things that I had and could do, and that nothing ever came without sacrifice.

Not for anyone.

I looked through the window of the store where we were and spotted a nice little shop right across the street.

A smile spread across my lips.

I loved combining different fun pieces and making new outfits. I could pretend that each piece had its own story, and I loved imagining what it was.

Of course, most of the time, I couldn't buy anything because my mom would lose her mind. According to her, I was blessed that I could buy super expensive clothes and brands—it didn't matter that most of that stuff seemed all the same and lifeless.

That was why I loved picturing myself as someone else. Someone free who didn't know anything about the mafia.

One of my family's guards got in my view, slamming me back to reality. Meeting someone and falling in love was impossible when I had at least four guards lurking around wherever I went and watching my every step.

Maybe I should stop deluding myself.

I couldn't change who I was or run away from it.

Ever.

I'd have to find my happiness within the confines of my own world.

I knew my mom wouldn't let me out of here if I didn't pick a dress for myself too, so I strode toward the other end of the store.

"I don't know when she'll grow up and realize that we're not like everyone else," my mom said in what was supposed to be a hushed voice, but I could hear her anyway.

"Mom, it'll be fine," Adelina said. "Once she gets married—"

I strode farther away from them until I couldn't make out what they were saying anymore.

I glanced at a few dresses, but I didn't know which one to choose.

No, that was a lie.

I knew which dress my mom and Adelina would pick, but I hated it. Why did my family believe mafia women had to look sexy all the damn time, like some pretty tokens that were for display only?

If we were already stuck with outdated practices like arranged marriages—okay, I could admit that finding someone to marry when your whole family was in the mafia was almost impossible—couldn't we at least wear normal clothes?

Couldn't we at least pick someone from within our own world to love and live with? But I supposed if I told my parents I wanted to marry some guard, they'd choke me with their bare hands.

If only I didn't love my dad, my mom, my sister, and my two little brothers so much, maybe I'd run away and try to make a life of my own. But I couldn't imagine my life without them.

I just couldn't.

I glanced over my shoulder at my sister.

She'd figured out everything so easily. Slipped into

the role of a dutiful wife and a mother to my baby nephew with so much ease that it seemed like something perfectly natural.

Hopefully, I'd figure out one day how to make my family proud like Adelina had done.

The ringing of a phone made us all look at one of the guards. He pressed his phone to his ear, his face serious.

My mom and Adelina focused back on the dresses, but I couldn't look away from the guard.

Something was wrong.

No one called the guards and interrupted them from doing their duty for no reason, so something had to be up.

I just didn't know what.

"Ma'am, we have to go. Now!" the guard said to my mom as he waved on the rest of the guards.

"Natalia, come," my mom said to me. "Let's go."

My mom and Adelina hurried to the exit, and I trailed after them.

"What's going on?" I asked the guard, who was right next to me, but he remained silent.

It was one more of those things that bugged me about this life.

When there was danger or something was happening, we were expected to obey and not ask any questions. We had to trust our guards that they'd keep us safe, and that was all.

"It doesn't matter, honey," my mom said as she got hold of my arm and tugged me with her. "Let them do their job. We'll be fine."

"Call me," Adelina shouted to my mom as she climbed into one of the SUVs.

There was no time to say goodbye. She had to go back to her husband. Who knew when we'd get to see each other again?

It was frustrating, especially if this whole situation wasn't an emergency. Maybe my dad simply needed my mom for some reason.

My skin crawled with anxiety. The guards' faces were unreadable as my mom and I got into the back seat of our car.

My mom offered me a smile as she reached out for my hand and squeezed my fingers.

I didn't know how she could stand it. For all we knew, something could've happened to my dad.

"How can you do that?" I asked. "What if—"

"Shh, honey. Don't worry. Our guards will keep us safe, and whatever it is that is going on, your dad will handle it. We can't do anything about it. Why waste everyone's time with unnecessary questions?"

Unnecessary questions? Really? But what if there was something we *could* do?

I chewed on the inside of my cheek as the car kept speeding.

It seemed like an eternity until the car pulled over in the driveway of my family's mansion. I didn't wait for the guards to open the doors for us. I jumped out of the car and raced inside.

My dad's men were rushing around and talking in loud voices, which was something I'd never seen before.

My throat constricted.

Something bad was going on, or they wouldn't look as if they were getting ready for a war.

"Natalia!" my mom called after me, but I was already racing upstairs, to my dad's office.

Luckily, the door to my dad's office was cracked open, and I pressed myself against the wall, straining my ears.

I immediately recognized my dad's voice and felt a brief relief that he was here and nothing had happened to him, but there was someone else in there with him.

His second-in-command, Leo.

"I fucked up," my dad said. "I should've known it was a trap."

"We couldn't have known he'd turn on us. There was no evidence—"

"It doesn't matter now. The Cavallaros are coming for us. We need to get out of here."

"I'm afraid all our safe houses have been compromised. The team is looking for—"

A gasp escaped my throat.

Maybe my dad didn't want me to know anything about his business because he didn't want to worry me with things I shouldn't be thinking about, but I'd heard of the Cavallaros.

Everyone had.

They were the most powerful family in the city. I'd heard my dad's men talk about them more than a few times.

One of them had said the Cavallaros had three times more men than my family did. If the Cavallaros were after us, that was bad.

Really, really bad.

"How did that happen?" my dad asked. "They weren't supposed to find out about any of that, despite the terrible deal I'd made."

"I wish I knew, but there's no time to figure it out," Leo said.

"It doesn't matter now either. What do I do?" A hint of desperation laced my dad's voice.

"A deal might be the only way out of this."

I had no idea what had happened, but it seemed like my dad had struck a deal with the wrong people, which had somehow provoked the Cavallaros to attack us.

"What can I offer them? If they wanted our territory, they would've tried to take it a long time ago."

"What about Pagani? Can't he help us?" Leo asked.

"I'm afraid not. Pagani signed a deal with the

Cavallaros a few years ago too. I'm not going to put my daughter's and my grandson's lives in danger for what might be a lost cause. How much time do we have?"

"Not much. But if it's in the Cavallaros interest for us to keep control of our territory, then they might be willing to make a deal. Maybe with an offering to make things right. You were played too. It's not like you wanted to offend them."

"I could offer them money and my help. I don't know what else there is they might want." My dad sighed. "But I know that if they take over our territory, they'll get too close to their biggest enemy, and I'm sure they don't want that kind of trouble."

"How about offering them your daughter?" Leo asked, and my heart skipped a beat. "Franco Cavallaro has two sons, and they're both unmarried. They need heirs to strengthen their rule."

"Give them my Natalia? No. I can't. She's not ready, and from what I heard, those boys aren't a good match for anyone."

"I don't think they'll agree to anything else because, as you said, they have everything, and they can always give our territory to someone else after they deal with us."

My heart thudded loudly in my chest, my palms getting sweaty. We were all going to die, weren't we?

Unless...

Unless I married one of Cavallaro's sons.

The choice seemed so simple, right?

Why let my dad fight the Cavallaros and lose who knew how many men? And it wasn't just about that.

We'd all lose in the end too. I couldn't watch my parents die. I couldn't watch my younger brothers die either.

Ciro was only fifteen, and Gabriel thirteen. My mom had suffered through multiple miscarriages after she had me. My dad's advisors had already suggested multiple times for him to find himself another wife who could give him heirs, but my dad hadn't wanted to hear about it.

He and my mom had done IVF so my brothers would be born. Both my mom and dad had sacrificed so much for our family. I knew that.

Adelina had done the same for a lucrative business deal between my dad and Pagani.

Now, it was my turn.

I pushed the door open, bursting into the room.

Leo's eyebrows shot up, and my dad's brow furrowed.

"Natalia, now's not the—" my dad started to say.

"I'll do it," I said. "I'll marry. I'm ready."

"Honey, I know you want to do the right thing, but the Cavallaros aren't very nice people."

"Then what are we going to do, Dad? I don't want

anything to happen to you, or to Mom, or to Ciro and Gabriel."

My dad pressed his lips into a tight line, watching me up and down, his dark eyes trained on me.

"It's still not too late," Leo said. "I can send the offer right away. If they respond favorably—"

"Honey, are you sure?" My dad stepped away from his desk and strode toward me.

"Yes, I am." I lifted my chin, even though I was anything but sure.

My dad looked at Leo. "Send the offer."

Leo nodded, and my dad wrapped his arms tightly around me.

Tears prickled the corners of my eyes as he held me close and pressed his lips against the top of my head.

Even though I shuddered at the thought of marrying a Cavallaro, I was sure it would all be worth it if my family remained safe and sound.

CHAPTER 2

Gianluca

I SHOULDN'T BE HERE.

Going after the Bonamontes was supposed to be an easy task for my father's men. A Cavallaro shouldn't be doing any of the dirty or dangerous work, at least according to my father, but where was the fun in that?

My motorcycle was faster anyway, and I could get to

one of the Bonamontes' stash houses before anyone else could.

My father hadn't told me what the Bonamontes had done to piss him off, but it didn't really matter. If he wanted them wiped out, we could wipe them out.

I zigzagged through the cars, and as I got closer to the house that was my target, I could see Bonamonte's men trying to get some things from the house into their cars.

Running away like rats.

Ridiculous.

Weren't they at least going to try to put up a fight? Or were they trying to get to their boss as soon as possible so they could protect him?

It didn't matter because whatever it was, they'd fail.

I pulled out my gun and aimed.

One of them spotted me and shouted. As I fired, they ran for cover, but I got one of them in the head.

The noise of engines behind me told me my father's men were going to be here very soon. I reached the end of the street and turned around, revving the bike.

I sped right toward the men who were crouched behind an SUV. When I pulled the trigger, they returned fire, but I was on the move, and none of their bullets got me.

The adrenaline was pumping through me, and everything seemed like in slow motion.

One of the men broke into a run toward the house, and I aimed at him.

At the last moment, I realized one thing.

If I wanted to hit him, I had to lean my bike to avoid crashing into the house and probably lose control of the bike.

Crash or fall.

Fuck it.

I pulled the trigger a second before my bike crashed to the ground. The guy I'd been aiming for went down like a log, but so did I.

Pain erupted through my side and arm as my body scraped against the ground.

A laugh escaped my throat anyway as more shots rang out.

"Sir, are you all right?" One of my father's men was instantly by my side.

"Yeah, whatever." I waved the guy off as I pushed myself up, ignoring the burning feeling on my skin.

Most of Bonamonte's men were down, and my father's men had one that was still alive cornered.

"Wait!" I yelled before they could put a bullet in him.

We still needed to find out where exactly Bonamonte and his family were hiding. We'd figured out most of their safe houses and stash houses, but we only had an inkling of the area where they might be.

Until the boss wasn't dead, this wasn't over.

My father's men parted as I strode toward Bonamonte's guy. He had his hands up, his back against the wall, his eyes too wide, fear evident in them.

He knew he was going to die.

He was waiting for it.

Anyone in his place would know it was coming.

"Where's your boss?" I asked as I stopped in front of him. "Where's his family?"

"I don't know," he stammered.

"You don't know?" I raised an eyebrow at him, and then I punched him so hard I heard his nose crack. "How about now?"

He cried out, blood spurting everywhere.

"Please! I don't know!" he shouted.

I grabbed him by the throat, squeezing so hard his eyes bulged as he wheezed for breath. "You don't want to lie to me. Trust me."

"I'm not! I swear," he choked out when I let go of him.

I punched him again.

And again.

Even as pain spread through my knuckles and arm, I didn't stop until he was on the ground.

"Please! I don't... I don't know."

I kicked him in the stomach.

Maybe he really didn't know anything. He was just a soldier.

Muscle. Probably hadn't even seen his boss.

But he'd signed up for this life, and he knew the risks.

"Sir!"

"What?" I snapped at the guy who came rushing toward me.

"Boss wants us to pull back."

"What?" I frowned. "My father wants us to pull back? Are you fucking kidding me?"

We were winning.

We were way stronger than the Bonamontes. Stopping now for no good reason was going to make us look weak. What the fuck was my father thinking?

"Those are our orders," the guy said, pulling out his phone and turning the screen to me.

Mission abort.

Fuck.

If I wanted to know what was going on, I'd have to ask my father.

"Give me your gun." I'd dropped mine somewhere.

The guy handed me his gun.

I aimed at the man on the ground.

"But sir, we're supposed to—"

I pulled the trigger before the guy could finish the sentence.

"Yes, I know. Mission abort." I flashed him a smile I knew didn't reach my eyes and handed him back his gun.

I headed back to my bike and got it off the ground.

MY FATHER'S VOICE COULD be heard all the way from the other side of the hallway. He and my older brother were in his office and clearly having a shouting match about something.

If I didn't know how much my father adored Bruno Franco—yes, the old bastard had wanted his firstborn to carry his name too—I'd be more interested in their conversation.

Whatever they were fighting about, my father was going to forgive his favorite son for all of it, no matter how bad it was.

No matter how incompetent my brother was or how many mistakes he'd made.

"I'm not getting married!" Bruno yelled.

"Yes, you are!" my father said.

I headed past the office and found myself face-to-face with Sebastiano. His arms were crossed in front of him as his brown eyes scanned me up and down.

His graying brown hair was ruffled, which meant he was upset enough to have raked his fingers through it multiple times.

He'd been my bodyguard ever since I was a child, but once I grew up, I'd started ditching him more and more, and that was something he didn't like but couldn't do anything about.

"Listening in on my father, huh?" My lips spread into a smile.

He lifted his finger in front of his lips. "This is your chance," he whispered.

I furrowed my brow. My chance to do what, exactly?

Go into my father's office so he could yell at me instead of at my brother? If he'd found out I'd gone after the Bonamontes, nothing my brother had done would seem worse.

"Your father wants to strike a deal with the Bonamontes. They're offering their daughter in marriage, and you know how much your father wants you and your brother to have heirs," Sebastiano said.

"Yeah, and he'll get my brother to marry her. He's the firstborn."

"But Bruno is refusing to marry or take any responsibility, and he's almost thirty. Your father is tired of waiting."

"What are you saying?"

"I'm saying you could offer to marry the Bonamonte

girl instead of your brother. Once you have an heir, your father will see what we've all already seen. He'll see you're the best choice to take over the family business."

If by *we*, he meant just the two of us, then maybe he was right.

My father was never willing to give me a chance to prove myself.

Maybe this was it.

Maybe this was exactly what I needed.

My brother could still ruin everything and agree, but why not give it a shot? What did I have to lose?

"Go in there," Sebastiano said, placing his hand on my arm and squeezing.

I winced because it was the arm I'd fallen on.

Worry creased Sebastiano's brow. "What have you done?"

"I'm not five. Fuck off."

Sebastiano shook his head at me like a disappointed father.

I strode to my father's office.

Bruno was still shouting.

He and my father were staring at each other with serious expressions on their faces. They were almost like carbon copies.

Dark brown hair, gray eyes, same height, same stubbornness.

"If Bruno doesn't want to marry Bonamonte's daughter, I will," I said as I entered.

My father's eyes briefly narrowed at me, and then he focused back on Bruno. "Have you changed your mind?"

Bruno shot me a glare as if I'd just ruined whatever plan he had, which only made my blood boil. He had it all.

Father had given him so many opportunities, and this was yet another one. Instead of being grateful, he was sneering.

Maybe Sebastiano was right, and my father would finally get tired of his precious son's antics.

Bruno never appreciated what he had.

Never.

Maybe I should just get a gun and solve my problem once and for all.

One bullet for my father.

One for my brother.

It would all be over.

I'd have everything I'd ever wanted. I'd be boss.

But that was too easy.

It wasn't how I wanted to achieve my goal, no matter how stupid that seemed.

"I'm not marrying anyone," Bruno said through his teeth.

"Are you out of your mind, boy? If you want to be boss, you need an heir."

Bruno's jaw tightened.

What the fuck was up with him? I didn't know why he refused to marry. It wasn't like doing that would change anything, except gain him even more of our father's favor.

But then again, he didn't know what it was like not to be in our father's favor, so maybe he didn't understand.

"And I told you, I'm not doing it," Bruno said. "You can't make me."

"Fine. Then Gianluca is the one who's getting married, and Bruno, I hope you'll wake up from whatever dream you have running in your head and snap back to reality. I don't know what the hell is wrong with you."

"Nothing's wrong with me," Bruno said and stormed through the door.

What the fuck was up with him? I doubted he'd fallen in love with some girl and that was the reason why he refused to marry. He wasn't the type of person who believed bullshit such as love existed.

My father let out a sigh, and then he inclined his head to me.

Was this really happening? Was my father finally going to see Bruno wasn't worthy of his attention?

I headed out.

Bruno was in the hallway, leaning against the wall, his eyes filled with fury.

"What the fuck are you doing?" he snapped at me. "Why do you want to marry?"

"And why you don't want to do it, huh?" I shot him a glare. "You know what? I don't give a fuck."

I brushed past him.

Maybe he'd gotten tired of everyone believing the lie that he was the perfect son and the perfect heir.

Whatever had gotten into him, I hoped it wouldn't pass because there was no way I was letting this chance go.

CHAPTER 3

Natalia

I RAN MY FINGERS OVER the white lace, trying hard not to think about what was coming, but it was impossible to forget.

Today was my wedding day.

I still couldn't believe it was really happening.

Everything from the moment I'd told my dad I was willing to marry to save our family and him telling me that the Cavallaros had accepted the offer seemed like a blur.

Now, as I stood in front of a mirror in my wedding dress, I took a deep, shuddery breath.

I was going to mess up everything, wasn't I?

A knock sounded on the door, and a moment later, my dad appeared in the doorway.

"Can I talk to you for a minute, honey?" A small smile coated his lips.

I gave him a nod, forcing my lips into a smile and curling my fingers into fists so he wouldn't see I was shaking from anxiety and anticipation.

"You look beautiful," he said, spreading his arms.

I let him pull me into an embrace. His lips brushed my forehead.

"I'm so proud of you," he said.

It was something I'd been waiting to hear for a very long time, but my mind couldn't quite process it at the moment, so I just kept smiling.

"Are you sure you want to do this?" he suddenly asked, placing his finger under my chin and looking straight into my eyes.

"Yeah, I am."

No, I absolutely didn't want to marry some guy I didn't know, but what choice did I have? My marriage was the only thing that could stop the Cavallaros from killing us all.

"Thank you," he said softly. "I'll leave you to get ready now."

I flashed him another smile.

Just as he opened the door, Adelina let out a gasp as she'd almost run into him.

"Dad! What are you doing here?" she said. "I still need to do Natalia's makeup, and we don't have much time left!"

"I told you we should've hired a makeup artist."

She waved her hand. "I'll do a better job. You'll see. Now please leave us."

"All right. All right." My dad let out a laugh.

Adelina closed the door after him, her eyes widening as she let out a sigh. I had a feeling she was hiding something, but I wasn't sure what it was.

She held a big bag in her hand, and I assumed it was makeup.

"I know we don't have much time," she said, lowering her voice. "But I brought something for you. Come."

She waved me over as she placed her bag on my bed and sat down next to it. I settled on the other side of the bag, careful of my dress.

"What's going on?" I asked.

"Shh!" She lifted her finger in front of her lips. "We can't have anyone overhear what I'm about to tell you. Did you already pack your bags?"

"Um, yeah." I glanced at the suitcases in the corner of the room.

As soon as I married Gianluca Cavallaro and the ceremony was over, I'd have to go with him to my new home.

His home.

My prison.

I was so not looking forward to that. I hadn't even seen a photo of my future husband. All I knew about him was that he was Franco Cavallaro's younger son and that he was almost five years older than me.

I had no idea if I should be glad about that or not, especially if the rumors about him being bloodthirsty and cruel were true.

"Then hide this in one of your suitcases." She pulled something out of her bag lightning-fast and shoved it into my hand.

It was a bottle of some kind, and when I read the label, my eyebrows shot up.

Lube?

"Hide it! Now!" Adelina hissed, almost pushing me off the bed while she kept glancing at the door.

A smile tugged at my lips as I got to my feet and imagined my mom getting in here and seeing what my sister had just given me.

Hey, Mom, Adelina just got me a bottle of lube for my wedding. Cute, right?

I stuffed the bottle in my suitcase, between my things.

Adelina tapped the bed with her hand, so I sat down again.

"Use it before your wedding night, or well, any night before he comes to you. Get yourself ready for him, and it will hurt less," she whispered. "It's also supposed to help you get pregnant quicker. I think it helped me. But don't let your husband see you're using it."

"Um." I didn't know what to say to that. "Thanks?"

"Oh, and don't forget to wear something sexy. Just lie down, relax, and let him do what needs to be done." She placed her hand over mine, and what was probably supposed to be an encouraging smile crossed lips. "You don't need to worry about anything."

I glanced at her, then at the window.

Throwing myself to my death sounded more pleasant than what she'd just described. But I had a duty to my family, and I was going to do my best to fulfill it.

"Do you love your husband?" I tilted my head at her.

"Of course I do," she blurted out, almost automatically.

"No, I mean, do you really love him?" I searched her eyes.

"He's okay."

But that wasn't what I was asking.

Silly me.

Love didn't matter. Not for us, anyway.

"I know how you feel," she said. "I was nervous on my wedding day too, and on my wedding night. But I got used to it, and I got Carlo. He's my world, and I don't need anything else."

Carlo. Her son.

I swallowed past the lump in my throat. Everyone expected me to give Gianluca a son, but what if I couldn't?

If he was really as sadistic as people said he was, would my child be in danger from him just by being born?

Wasn't it sort of cruel to condemn another person to the mafia life? Because once you were born into it, there was no way out, except death.

Just thinking about it all seemed surreal, and as if it were happening to someone else and not to me.

I supposed I should be grateful my dad hadn't married me off as soon as I'd turned eighteen, and I'd gotten to enjoy my carefree life for a few years longer.

"You know what will be fun?" Adelina said.

"What?"

"Once you have a son, he and Carlo will play together, and you and I will talk over tea." A wide smile popped up on her lips. "We'll be so happy. You'll see. It'll all be worth it."

I nodded, but I couldn't feel as excited about it as she was.

Who knew if my husband would even let me see my family. My sister made the whole thing sound so easy and simple, as if she could actually see the future, but I knew the reality was very different.

Adelina glanced at the watch on her wrist. "Crap! You need to get ready. Get in that chair! Now!"

"Can't I just stay here?" I patted the bed.

"No."

I pushed myself up and then settled in the chair in front of my dressing table. Adelina pulled out a makeup kit.

"Do you think it's true?" I asked as she picked up a brush.

"What?"

"What they say about Gianluca."

She furrowed her brow. "I don't know what you mean."

"Well, didn't you hear about it? That he's a monster? That he doesn't care about anyone or anything? That he gets off on his enemies' pain?"

She blinked at me. "No, I don't think that's true. You know how mafia guys are. They just want everyone to think they're super bad and super dangerous."

"But most of them *are* super bad and super dangerous."

"You're going to be his wife. He's bound to protect

you. Who cares what he does with his enemies? You won't have to see or deal with any of that."

"Yeah, I guess you're right."

"Of course I'm right. Now close your eyes so I can put some eye shadow on you."

I did as she asked.

Maybe she was right. Maybe there was nothing to worry about.

Or maybe I'd be walking on eggshells for the rest of my life.

But even if Gianluca was the biggest of monsters, marrying him to save my family would still be worth it.

How many times had I said that to myself already? Had it finally become true?

"Open your eyes," Adelina said.

I did.

She gave me a big smile. "Perfect. Now let me put your hair up."

"I don't want it up," I said.

"But you need to have it up because of the veil."

"Right."

Was there even going to be anything left of me in all this? I was wearing a dress my mom had chosen. Yeah, it was a pretty dress, but it wasn't what I would've picked.

I'd be someone else today.

Or maybe this was all a sign that I had to let go of the real me and start pretending.

Smile.

Be pretty.

Do your duty.

Hope your husband will finally leave so you can have a tiny bit of freedom in your prison.

I looked around my room, at my bed, my closet, my shelf full of books, my favorite teddy bear on my nightstand...

Maybe I didn't want to admit it to myself just yet, but my life was over.

I had to finally grow up, no matter how scary that seemed or how much I wanted to postpone it for a bit longer.

All I could do now was treasure my happy memories of all the special moments I'd spent with my family here and hope they'd keep me warm forever.

The door suddenly burst wide open.

"I got it!" my brother, Ciro, shouted as he lifted his hand with his phone.

There was a huge smile on his face, his dark eyes sparkling with joy, but I was sure Mom wasn't going to like that his brown hair was a complete mess.

"You got it? You got the pic?" Adelina turned to him with interest.

"I told you I would." Ciro grinned.

"Let me see." Adelina rushed to him.

I furrowed my brow as they kept grinning while staring at the screen of my brother's phone.

"What's going on?" I asked.

"Holy..." Adelina muttered. "He's hot."

"Who's hot? Come on, don't make me get up again. I'll ruin the dress." I groaned.

Adelina approached with a huge smile on her face and turned the phone screen to me.

It was a photo of a guy. A very good-looking guy.

Jet-black hair. Piercing blue eyes. He was wearing a suit, but I could tell he was tall, lean, and probably muscular.

He had to be an actor, a model, or something.

"That's Gianluca Cavallaro," Adelina said.

My jaw went slack. "You're messing with me."

"No, I'm not. That's him."

"It is." Ciro bobbed his head.

"Huh." I stared at the image, but Gianluca's face was unreadable.

Was he the monster everyone said he was?

Him being hot meant absolutely nothing, except that women were probably throwing themselves at him all the time, so he might not have as much interest in me.

Would that be a good thing?

I was going to find out soon enough.

CHAPTER 4

Gianluca

I GROANED AS I GOT out of my car and my gaze landed on the garden where my wedding was going to take place.

Everything had been set up—the chairs, the red carpet leading to the wedding arch, the white bows, hearts and flowers—as if Natalia Bonamonte and I were getting married like regular people.

I hadn't even seen my bride, and I'd refused when Sebastiano had offered to show me a photo of her so I wouldn't change my mind.

The whole thing was unnecessary.

A waste of everyone's time.

I had no idea who my father and the Bonamontes had invited to the wedding, but Natalia and I could've just signed the marriage certificate and be done with it.

Why go through the whole ceremony when we could be doing more important things?

But my father didn't agree, so we were all forced to be here.

I spotted Bruno in the distance. He had a scowl on his face when he saw me.

I still had no idea what the fuck his deal was. If he'd wanted to marry Natalia, he could have, so why was he pissed at me?

He must've been plotting something, but he wasn't going to tell me what it was.

It didn't matter, because I had my own plan, and I wasn't going to fail.

Sebastiano approached, his brow creasing.

"What?" I asked because he was staring at my tie.

"It's your wedding. Everything needs to be perfect," he said, then started adjusting my tie.

"Who cares about my fucking tie?" I'd never felt comfortable wearing ties.

I preferred not to wear one or have it very loose if it was required.

"Everyone except you." Sebastiano's lips spread into a smile as he stepped away from me. "There. It's better now."

"Whatever. When is this going to be over?"

"It hasn't even started."

"I need a drink." I strode past Sebastiano to find the table with drinks.

There had to be one.

Once I spotted it, my lips pulled up into a smile. I picked up a bottle of whiskey and glanced at the label.

Good stuff.

Perfect.

I opened the bottle and took a big gulp.

Then I spotted my father and Bruno talking under one of the trees.

I clenched my jaw.

What was my brother trying to do now? Ruin the whole thing? If he'd changed his mind about the wedding, would Father just let him take my place?

Was that even a question?

Of course he would.

I took another swig from the bottle.

My father clapped Bruno on the shoulder, and then he headed toward me.

My shoulders tensed as I placed the bottle back on the table.

My father's face was serious, his eyes hard as he scanned me up and down, as if he was looking for an imperfection.

But that wasn't anything new. He was always looking for something I'd done wrong. Something I was missing. Just so he could tell me Bruno was better at it.

"The ceremony will start soon," he said. "Don't fuck it up."

He gave me another cold look and walked away from me.

Don't fuck it up?

What could I possibly fuck up? It was just a fucking wedding.

I reached for the bottle again, but Sebastiano grabbed it before I could.

"All the guests are here," he said.

"Right," I muttered and headed to the spot where I was supposed to stand and wait for my bride.

The guests were murmuring and chattering too much, and I didn't know most of them. My mother was sitting next to my father, her head—with a huge pink hat that matched her dress—bowed.

I hadn't seen her for months, which wasn't unusual at all because she'd been absent and kept away in some safe house for most of my life.

When her blue eyes finally lifted to mine, she smiled, and I looked away. She was like a stranger to me.

Just another person who'd had to come here to witness this charade.

The music started—my father had hired an orchestra—and I focused my gaze on Bonamonte as he led his daughter toward me.

A huge veil covered her face, and her dress full of lace wasn't any better. All I could tell about her so far was that she was of average height.

When she stopped across from me, my gaze fell on her hands. Her fingers were shaking.

Was it anxiety or something else? Was she afraid of me?

Once the officiant had yapped away whatever the hell he was supposed to say, and I said *I do*, Natalia hesitated.

Her *I do* was so soft that it was barely audible.

Either she was having second thoughts about the whole thing, or there was something wrong with her. Had my father even checked if she was healthy?

We even had to exchange the rings, and her grip was firmer when she slid the ring on my finger.

It was finally the time to find out if I'd married the ugliest woman in the whole world.

I lifted the veil.

My eyebrows briefly shot up, my lips parting in

surprise.

Big dark brown eyes stared back at me.

Fuck.

She was beautiful.

I'd gotten lucky. Fucking her wasn't going to be a problem at all. I placed my hand on her cheek and pulled her to me, pressing my mouth against her soft, full lips.

She let out a small gasp.

Her cheeks were flushed too.

So innocent and sweet, but she wouldn't be for long.

I was going to enjoy having some fun with her until she got pregnant. Hopefully, she'd give me an heir by the time I got bored with her—and I always got bored, no matter how pretty the woman was.

Once her purpose was fulfilled, I could send her away somewhere and never see her again, unless I needed another heir.

But a son should be enough for my father to see that I was a far better candidate for leadership than my brother would ever be.

If Bruno didn't want to have a wife or any heirs, there was no way my father could ever overlook that and forgive him. Without heirs, our family legacy couldn't be continued.

I didn't know what Bruno was thinking, but his stupidity was helping me this time.

As I took hold of my wife's hand, I put a big smile on my face as everyone cheered and clapped.

I started toward my brother on purpose just so I could see the look on his face once he realized I hadn't only successfully done exactly what Father expected of us but that my wife was also one of the hottest women he and I had ever seen.

When I looked at my father, he gave me a small nod, the corners of his lips tilted up. I couldn't remember if he'd ever done that before.

He was usually scowling at me or expressing his displeasure in some way.

My gaze locked with Bruno's. His face was serious, his jaw tense. His gaze fell on Natalia, and something flashed in his eyes.

Yes, brother, be envious.

Be very, very envious.

Because this game has only just started, and I'm already winning.

Your move, brother.

CHAPTER 5

Natalia

I PACED UP AND DOWN my new room. If the situation were different, I'd be in love with this house.

It was a huge mansion, surrounded by thick woods. It had a beautiful yard full of flowers and a pool.

Everything in every room was perfectly arranged, a mix of modern and old. The white and black marble floor glistened in the light coming from the elaborate crystal chandeliers. The furniture was mostly in white and dark blue tones, and everything was spotless.

My room was very spacious, and I had my own private bathroom, which was also huge and contained both a shower and a bathtub.

There was a huge closet, a beautiful, white dressing table carved with roses, and a door that led to a balcony. The windows were huge and allowed plenty of light from the outside to get in.

My king-sized bed was impossibly soft, with a bunch of dark blue pillows, and silk dark blue covers.

My things had already been brought here, and all I had to do was unpack.

My husband was even more handsome in person than in that photo of him that I'd seen.

And yet...

Despite everything appearing perfect, I knew it was far from that.

I was in a new house, which wasn't my home and which was surrounded by more than a dozen armed guards and an electric fence. There was no one for miles around here to help me if I needed it.

If I'd been nervous at the wedding, now I was on the brink of losing my mind.

The way Gianluca had looked at me once he lifted my veil and when his lips had crashed against mine...

I still didn't know what to think about him. He hadn't said a word to me on our way here.

Everything was all new and scary to me.

I'd never been away from my family like this.

I couldn't even see a phone anywhere so I could try to call my sister and ask her for advice. She'd already told me everything I needed to know, and it wasn't like I was clueless about what my role and purpose here was, or what needed to be done.

Hell, I'd signed up for it of my own free will.

But my throat was constantly tight and dry, and not even a gulp of water helped. My stomach churned, but I wasn't hungry.

I sat down on the bed and lowered my head into my hands.

Just knowing that everything now depended on me not messing things up drove me crazy.

I wasn't like my sister. I didn't even know if I was ready for any of this.

Gianluca would come to my room later for our wedding night, and I had no idea how I was supposed to make love to a stranger.

No, not make love. We weren't in love, obviously.

We'd never be.

It would just be sex.

I took a deep breath and slowly released it.

A shower.

I needed a shower to calm my nerves. Maybe I didn't have any real experience with sex, but I knew I had to be as relaxed as possible, not like this.

I hopped to my feet to find something to change into. I was still in my wedding dress, and a part of me was actually glad Gianluca had had the servants show me to my room and that they'd left me alone.

But once I stood under the warm stream of water, I closed my eyes and fought the urge to cry. What the hell was wrong with me?

I'd always known I'd have to marry someone from the mafia and that I most likely wouldn't know them.

I was doing this to save my family. Women in my family had done it for decades. So why did I feel like I wanted to jump out of my skin?

Maybe I should ask one of the servants for a glass of something strong, but I didn't think Gianluca would want a drunk bride.

For a second, I considered doing just that so the whole wedding night would be postponed, but would Gianluca do that? Would he even care if I was out of it?

No, I couldn't do that.

Shit! I needed to be clearheaded.

What had Adelina said that I had to do?

I got out of the shower and wrapped a towel around myself.

Something sexy.

I was supposed to wear something sexy.

I dug through my suitcase, trying to find my nightgown.

The pink one?

I lifted it up and glanced at the mirror.

Nope. Too sweet.

The black one?

Nope.

It was like I was going to a Halloween party or something—not that I'd ever been allowed to do anything like that, but I'd seen it in movies.

Red one?

I groaned. Too sexy.

Maybe me thinking that meant it was just the perfect one, but I didn't want to put it on.

The white one?

I bit down on my lip, tilting my head at my reflection in the mirror.

That should be fine, right?

It was like my wedding dress. Not too sexy, but not too plain either.

I glanced through the window. It was already getting dark, which meant Gianluca would probably come soon.

Where was he now? What was he doing?

Definitely not freaking out like I was.

As I was putting on the nightgown, I paused.

Should I put on some underwear? Or would that just be in the way?

Damn. I was worse than a teenage girl trying to pick what to wear on her first date.

But then again, I hadn't even been on any dates ever, and yet here I was, married.

How was I supposed to pick something my husband was going to like when I knew absolutely nothing about what he liked?

What was his favorite color? Judging by a whole lot of dark blue in this house, I'd say definitely dark blue, but I didn't have any dark blue nightgowns.

Did it even matter? He was only supposed to have sex with me to get me pregnant, so maybe it didn't.

Like my sister had said, he'd come, do the deed, and leave.

It would be fine.

I'd survive.

If I got lucky or unlucky—I wasn't sure yet—I wouldn't immediately get pregnant.

A normal girl of my age would probably think I sounded like a childish idiot, but she wasn't the one who'd missed out on pretty much most of normal people's experiences. It had been who'd lived my life sheltered from the world.

I'd been homeschooled, so I'd never even had a crush

or anything. My mom or my guards had always watched my every move.

Even browsing the internet had been limited because my father's men monitored everything that happened on my family's special secure network—the only times when I'd been exposed to something I wasn't supposed to see was when a weird ad popped up, or if it was one of those articles about sex that were sometimes published on teen websites.

All the movies and TV shows I'd watched had been preapproved by my mom.

Every single aspect of my life had been controlled by someone from my family, and now my husband would take on that role, and I didn't even know what to expect of him.

Would he be like Enrico?

Would he be worse?

I had to stop thinking about that because it would only make me more miserable. If I kept acting weird like this, Gianluca could change his mind about me, and then the deal with my family would be over.

I couldn't let that happen.

Maybe I could find a friend in this house—one of the staff girls. Someone who could tell me more about Gianluca and would help me find my place in this house.

Someone who could assure me that Gianluca would

be a good father. Knowing that he would be kind to our future child would alleviate at least some of my fears.

As I stuffed my things back into my suitcase—I was in no state of mind to unpack now—the bottle of lube my sister had given me caught my eye.

I should follow her advice. She knew what she was doing, unlike me. My hand closed around the bottle, but then I put it back.

It was too weird.

I couldn't do it.

Maybe next time.

If sex really ended up hurting that much.

Oh hell.

I ran my hand through my hair.

Was Gianluca going to like my long dark brown hair that came all the way to the middle of my back, or was he going to order me to cut it shorter? Maybe even get me to dye it?

Before Adelina had gotten pregnant, Enrico had made her bleach her hair so it would be even lighter because he preferred blondes. Now that she'd given him a son, he apparently didn't care, so she was back to her natural light brown.

Except, I didn't want to change my hair color or style.

I let out a groan of frustration and sat down on the bed. Should I be sitting or lying down when he came for me?

Should I lower my nightgown's strap down my shoulder?

Should I look more innocent or more inviting?

Why didn't marriage come with a manual? My task was to please my husband, and yet, I had no idea what the hell he even wanted. I wasn't a mind reader.

Adelina would tell me that I was overthinking the whole thing, and she'd be right.

I was freaking out over the inevitable, and it had to stop.

My worry wasn't going to change anything.

Thinking about it a billion times wasn't going to help either.

I just had to let it happen and hope for the best.

CHAPTER 6

Gianluca

SEBASTIANO WAS OUTSIDE in the yard on his phone, his brow creased. Something was wrong, and I wanted to know what.

Since I wasn't the one who'd received the call, Sebastiano had to be talking to one of his spies, and that was never good because, in most cases, it was related to my brother.

When he slipped his phone into the pocket of his pants, I headed toward him.

"What's up?" I asked, eyeing him carefully.

"Nothing." His eyebrow twitched.

"I expect many people to lie to my face, but not you." I crossed my arms. "Is it about Bruno?"

Sebastiano sighed. "Yes, and no."

"What do you mean?"

"It's nothing to worry about. It's your wedding night. We'll talk about it tomorrow."

I shook my head. "I can fuck my wife whenever I want. You're not going anywhere until you tell me what you found out."

"Your father sent Bruno to deal with the Vinicellis. They've been causing some trouble—"

"What?" I spat out. "After everything that happened, he sent my brother to do it?"

"It doesn't mean anything. Like I said, your father doesn't want to ruin your wedding night. Your wife needs to get pregnant as soon as possible. An heir is worth way more than some small mission."

I bared my teeth. "The Vinicellis are at the edge of my fucking territory. Mine! What the fuck does Bruno know about them? I know where they're hiding. I know how to find them. I know almost all of their members. He's going to fuck things up! I need to call my father and—"

"No, wait!" Sebastiano said. "Don't. Not tonight. Let

your brother handle the Vinicellis. If he fails, all the better. Your father's patience will run out."

"What if *my* patience runs out? I'm done being in Bruno's shadow. If my father can't see my brother isn't fit to lead anyone after everything he's done, then he never will, and I'm wasting my fucking time."

"You're not wasting your time. You're doing exactly what you're supposed to. Just give it a bit more time. Make sure your wife gives you an heir."

"You know I can't just snap my fingers and make that happen."

"Yes, I'm aware. That's why you need to start tonight. With some luck, you'll have everything you've ever wanted within a year."

Luck.

Ridiculous.

"Look, if things don't work out with Natalia, you can find someone else and—"

"No. My father would see it as my failure, and he'd be right."

"He doesn't have to find out. If you had a son with a lover, Natalia wouldn't have a choice but to accept the child as hers and never say a word about it to anyone."

I gave him a deadpan look. "My father always finds out, and if he did, he'd never forgive me for tricking him like that. And you know he doesn't want our blood mixing with random people. I doubt I'd find a girl from a respectable mafia family dumb enough to secretly get pregnant with me and risk everything."

"Yeah, you're right." Sebastiano's face was pensive. "Don't think about it right now. Everything's going to work out. You and Natalia are both young and healthy, and there shouldn't be any problems. You'll see. Even if things don't work out as we planned, we'll come up with something, or Bruno will drive the last nail into his coffin all on his own."

I nodded, and headed back inside.

I had to fuck my wife, and I was looking forward to it. She was hot, and I hoped she wouldn't be boring in bed.

I strode straight to Natalia's room. When I opened the door, she let out a gasp, her eyes wide and startled. I should've knocked first.

She was sitting on the pillows in a white nightgown, her fingers curled in the fabric as if her life depended on it.

Fuck.

This wasn't going to be as easy as I'd expected. Her shoulders were too tense, her chest rapidly rising and falling.

Maybe innocence was a turn-on for someone, but not for me. Maybe for someone who liked to make love, not fuck. Or for someone who found fear and reluctance appealing.

Natalia tried to cover her nervousness up with a smile, but it looked way too forced.

"Are you a virgin?" I asked as I closed the door behind me.

"Yes, of course."

Ah, fuck.

No wonder she looked like a deer caught in the headlights.

I shouldn't be surprised. Mafia women were different from the women I usually fucked and who knew nothing about me or about my world.

But there might be a solution to my problem.

I pulled out my phone. A few taps later, I had exactly what I needed. A smile spread across my lips.

I tossed the phone to Natalia. She caught it with a surprised look on her face.

"I'm going to take a shower," I said. "You take a look at the videos on the phone and pick one that turns you on the most. Pick what you want me to do to you. And get rid of that nightgown. I want you naked."

She gaped at me and kept glancing between me and the phone.

"Yeah, okay," she finally said.

I watched her for a moment, wondering what it was going to take for her to let go of the sweet, innocent mafia princess that had to keep her desires and wants under strict control.

Was there fire inside her?

Or ice?

Maybe Natalia's innocence wasn't as boring as I'd first thought but more like a challenge.

I had to discover the real her.

Unwrap her.

Unfold her secrets.

Would I like what I uncovered?

Or would fucking her become a chore?

I'd find out soon enough.

CHAPTER 7

Natalia

MY EYES BULGED AS GIANLUCA pulled his shirt over his head, revealing his toned chest. I quickly lowered my gaze to the phone in my hand, but curiosity prevailed and I glanced at Gianluca again.

He yanked down his pants and underwear, and I let

out a gasp as something like a current of electricity zapped through my body.

Damn, his body was perfection.

He turned toward me, and my gaze lowered to his cock.

My mouth fell open.

He was huge. How was all that supposed to fit—

I quickly focused on the phone again, even though it felt extremely stupid to avoid looking at my naked husband as if it was wrong.

I stole another glance of his ass and back as he made his way to my bathroom, and I bit down on my lip.

When he closed the door after him, I blinked.

What had he said about me choosing a video of what I wanted him to do to me? Was there actually a manual for this after all that no one had told me about?

I brought the screen back to life and tapped the first video. A yelp escaped my throat when I realized what the video was.

Naked people.

Having sex.

My eyes were glued to the screen as I watched the video.

No.

Nope.

I couldn't do that.

I stopped the video and opened another one.

The man in it kissed his way down the woman's body and buried his head between her legs.

A surge of warmth filled my insides.

Would Gianluca really do that if I wanted him to?

I switched to another video.

My hand flew to my mouth as the scenes played out in front of my eyes. The heat between my legs intensified.

Why did I like what I was seeing so much? Everything I'd been taught over the years told me that I should be ashamed just for watching this, but I didn't feel that way.

I was all hot and bothered, and I wasn't sure what I was supposed to do with it. What if this was a test? What if Gianluca was playing with me?

Adelina had never talked about anything like this, and she definitely hadn't mentioned any videos, but maybe that would be too much to discuss with your sister anyway.

I checked out another video, but I already knew which one was my favorite.

Should I try to figure out which one was Gianluca's favorite? Would this stuff even feel as good as it felt just watching it?

I inwardly groaned.

I was so done with doubting my every move and every single thing I said.

It was hard to forget my upbringing and all those times my mom had told me my purpose was to support my husband in everything and go along with everything he asked of me.

But Gianluca had asked me to pick a video, so that was what I was going to do.

My shoulders had relaxed a fraction.

Everything was going to be fine.

Wait, my nightgown.

I was supposed to take it off. As I pulled it over my head, I released a small breath. Goosebumps rose on my skin because the air seemed cold compared to my heated flesh.

The bathroom door opened, and Gianluca strolled out.

My lips parted. His hair was damp, and a few drops of water were gliding down his muscular body.

Oh hell.

His eyes traveled my body, and I fought the urge to cover myself. No one had ever seen me naked like this.

No one had ever looked at me the way he was doing it now. Something flashed in his eyes—like hunger—as his gaze explored every inch of my body.

His cock seemed even bigger now.

Hard.

Another shot of electricity went straight through my core.

"Which one?" he asked.

I licked my dry lips, picked up the phone, and tapped my finger over the video. When I placed the phone in his outstretched hand, I didn't look away from his face, but it was pointless because he was giving me nothing.

Whatever he was thinking or feeling, it was hidden behind a perfectly composed expressionless mask.

"Are you sure?" His gaze lifted to me as he placed the phone on the dressing table.

"Yes."

He narrowed his eyes, as if he didn't believe me. "Spread your legs. I want to see you."

I lay back on the pillows to get more comfortable as I lifted my knees and slowly pushed my legs open.

Gianluca didn't look away from me, and even though I'd expected I'd feel ashamed about him seeing me like this, I didn't.

The air got even hotter around me, or maybe it was just my body that was heating up.

"Wider," Gianluca said as he climbed on the bed.

I obeyed.

He inched closer, his eyes on me.

His hand lowered toward my leg, but instead of touching me, he kept it hovering just above my skin.

"You ready?" he asked.

I gave him a small nod.

His fingers touched my skin, and he ran them up my leg. His other hand landed on my other leg.

"I've never fucked a virgin before," he said, his eyes meeting mine. "If you want me to stop or anything feels uncomfortable, you need to tell me."

"Okay," I said softly.

His fingers kept gliding over my skin, up and down.

He flashed me a smile before lowering his lips to my inner thigh. A soft gasp escaped me as his lips moved over my skin, getting closer and closer to my center.

When his mouth pressed against my core, I tensed.

But when his tongue darted out and slid across my opening, pushing against my folds, every single bit of hesitation, doubt, or anxiety vanished as if it had never existed.

His tongue teased and toyed with me, flicking over my clit in the most wonderful ways, and my insides throbbed with a need unlike anything I'd ever felt before.

Gianluca's fingers dug into my thighs as he lapped at me, his tongue pushing in and out and driving me crazy.

I let out a loud moan as his tongue circled my clit, and every inch of my body was on fire, needing and begging for more.

He squeezed my thighs even harder, his tongue bringing me closer and closer to the edge.

I cried out as a wave of pleasure overcame me so

strongly that it spread through my whole body, leaving me breathless.

Gianluca moved up my body then, his hands and his mouth exploring and inspecting. He cupped my breast, kneading hard.

His fingers pinched my nipple as his mouth closed around the other, and a pang of pain quickly melted away into pleasure.

Oh hell.

What he was doing to my body was beyond anything I could've possibly imagined. Maybe I knew what to expect because I'd seen the video, but seeing something was completely different from actually experiencing it.

From feeling it.

I gasped, the fire inside me roaring, as Gianluca's teeth grazed my nipple. He sucked and tugged, sending all kinds of amazing sensations through me.

He pushed himself up, grabbing my wrists and pinning them on each side of my head. His gaze met mine as he kept me trapped under his strong body.

His cock rubbed against me once, twice, eliciting another moan from the depths of my throat.

He plunged inside me, filling me and stretching me until he was buried deep inside me. I let out a surprised yelp at the new sensations, but any discomfort I might have felt disappeared very quickly.

He didn't move, just watched me, letting me get used to him.

And then he almost pulled out, only to slam himself back inside so fast and hard that I cried out.

He tightly gripped my wrists as he pumped in and out of me, his thrusts merciless. My breath came out in little puffs, and my body vibrated with ecstasy.

His lips collided with mine as he pounded into me.

It was as if he was everywhere.

Around me.

Inside me.

Taking and possessing every atom of my being.

And I liked it.

Another deep and powerful thrust spilled me over, shattering my bubble of pleasure into a billion pieces that spread through my body.

Gianluca groaned, shoving himself into me once again, prolonging my release, which pulsated through me as he throbbed inside me.

He kissed me, still keeping me pinned to the bed. His gaze met mine, and then his lips spread into a small smile.

When he let go of me and rolled off me, I was still trying to catch my breath.

I'd never thought sex would feel so good, and a part of me already wanted to try another thing I'd seen in one of those videos.

Gianluca's face got serious as he rose to his feet and started getting dressed. I pulled the covers over me, watching him carefully.

What now? Was he just going to leave? We had separate rooms, but that was nothing unusual.

My parents didn't share a room either because my dad didn't want to wake up my mom when he got home late or when he had to go somewhere urgently in the middle of the night.

"You can keep the phone," Gianluca said as he pulled on his shirt. "I'll get myself another one. It has access to the database of all the numbers you might need, including your family's. Secure network, of course."

"Um, thanks."

Without another word, he headed to the door.

I bit down on my lip.

I had no idea what I'd been expecting.

Why would he stay? We'd done what we were supposed to do, and that was that.

I just wish I didn't feel so weird about it now.

Used, somehow.

As if there was something more that I'd wanted and that hadn't happened.

And all because he hadn't stayed for at least a bit longer.

As I grabbed one of the pillows and hugged it tightly,

I noticed my wrists were red where Gianluca had held me.

The high I'd felt was wearing off, and the soreness between my legs intensified, but I still didn't have any regrets about choosing what I'd chosen.

I glanced at the phone.

Should I call Adelina or my mom? I wanted to, but they'd probably get worried because it was so soon.

My sister had called me about a week after she got married and left with her husband. I didn't want my family to worry that something was already wrong or that I'd messed things up.

No, I'd call them later.

I'd be fine.

I'd survived the first night, and I'd survive all the others too.

And maybe I'd even look forward to them.

CHAPTER 8

Gianluca

THERE WAS HOPE FOR my wife. She might not be boring after all, but she had to get out of her comfort zone first.

Even now as I pictured the rise of her breasts and the curve of her ass, I was getting hard again. Something like that had never happened before.

I usually fucked a woman and forgot all about her. Never seen her again. Never fucked anyone twice.

But Natalia was my wife, which was different. She knew exactly who I was, and there was no need for me to pretend or disappear from her life before she could even remember my name.

Still, it was strange that I was thinking about her at all. I hadn't seen that coming.

Judging by the look on her face, she'd had her first orgasm last night. That thought made me smile, even though I'd never cared about being anyone's first. Actually, I hated the idea of having someone inexperienced with me.

Natalia was just different. Her innocence intrigued me, and I couldn't wait for her to discover what else she liked.

For her shyness to disappear completely.

"I've been looking for you," Sebastiano said as soon as he spotted me from the end of the hallway.

"Why? What's up?" Usually, I'd be up early in the morning and focusing on business, but today wasn't that day.

"It's Bruno. His mission failed. The Vinicellis forced him to pull back."

I let out a throaty laugh. "Seriously? Well, that's some amazing news. I knew that was going to happen. I should've been the one to deal with the Vinicellis. Does my father finally see that?"

"Your father is disappointed, of course." Sebastiano hesitated.

I pressed my lips tightly together. "Let me guess. He still doesn't plan on calling me to do something about the Vinicellis."

"You've just gotten married and—"

"And that's a lame excuse!" I snapped. "What is my father waiting for, huh? That the Vinicellis start thinking we're all incompetent and that they can defeat us without a problem? Doesn't he see Bruno is ruining our reputation?"

"I'm sure your father's patience with your brother is running out."

"I'm not."

Even though none of this surprised me, it still enraged me every damn time. In the end, I'd have to give up my family values and take what I wanted by force.

"Everything's going well so far," Sebastiano said. "Don't forget that. You have a wife and soon you'll have an heir. Your father won't have a choice but to send you to take care of the Vinicellis, and then your brother will fall out of favor."

"Right." I wished I were my father's first call when something came up.

Just once.

So what if I wasn't firstborn?

I was a better choice, and no one could deny it.

Except, my father would try, no doubt.

"Do you think our prisoner knows something about the Vinicellis and what they might be planning?" My blood was pumping through my veins with fury, and I needed something to make me feel better about this whole thing.

"I don't think so."

"Bring him to me." I didn't have to tell him where I wanted our prisoner to be.

Sebastiano knew full well about the empty room that we used for interrogation since the dungeon in the basement wasn't big enough and the floors weren't as easy to clean.

His brow furrowed. "Are you sure you want to do that now?"

"That was an order. I don't need your advice." I cracked my knuckles.

Sebastiano opened his mouth, but then he closed it and inclined his head.

Better.

Once he was gone, I strode to the interrogation room. I entered the dim, empty space and rolled the sleeves of my dress shirt up.

The guards brought a dark-haired guy with wide

dark eyes inside. The guy was in chains and struggling. I'd forgotten his name.

I thought it was Mark, or something like that.

Not that it mattered.

The guards pushed him down to his knees in the middle of the room and attached his chains to the hooks on the floor so that he wouldn't be able to escape or move too much.

"Please," Mark said. "Please let me go. I don't know anything. I won't tell anyone anything about you. Please! Have mercy."

Mercy.

I stood above him, just watching him beg and cry. His clothes were dirty and torn, his hair caked and crusted with dried blood. I couldn't even remember when and why we'd picked him up.

Ah, yes.

He'd been spying on me during one of my missions, and my men hadn't gotten him to talk since he claimed he'd only found himself in the wrong place at the wrong time.

I didn't believe him.

"You work for the Vinicellis, don't you?" I asked.

"I don't know who that is!"

"Liar." I kicked him hard in the stomach.

He doubled over with a cry of pain. "No. I swear I don't know them!"

I kicked him again, and again. "Do you really expect me to believe you just happened to lurk in the darkest corner of an abandoned factory in the middle of the night? And not on any night, but exactly the night I showed up. Almost like someone tipped you off. Someone who somehow found out where I'd be, or maybe someone had a good guess about it."

"I've been there before! Just looking for—"

I crouched, burying my fingers into his hair and yanking hard. "I hate lies. There's a camera close by. You can see the whole factory from there, so I know you haven't been there before."

I shoved him back to the floor.

"I... I..." His chest heaved as he was probably trying to come up with another lie.

Pathetic.

I punched him hard in the face, blood spurting from his nose. He let out a cry, and I punched him again.

My knuckles hurt, and light pain spread through my hand as I kept hitting him. It made me feel a tiny bit better, especially if I imagined Bruno's face instead.

I lost myself in the sounds of punches and rhythmic movements.

Mark's moans and groans grew louder, and there was blood everywhere.

A shadow caught my eye, and I lifted my gaze.

Natalia stood in the hallway, right in front of the

door, which was cracked open. Unlike the guards with their expressionless faces, her eyes were impossibly wide as she stared at me, her lips parted.

As if she was looking straight at a monster.

I jerked back, getting to my feet and looking down at my bloody hands.

It was as if she'd just ripped me out of a different world.

A different existence.

What was that in her eyes?

Disgust? Fear?

What the fuck was I even doing?

What was she doing here?

Why did it bother me that she'd seen me like this? It wasn't like she didn't know who I was and what I did.

I started toward her, but she spun on her heel and disappeared from view.

What was I even going to tell her with all the blood on my hands? I couldn't go after her like this.

Fuck!

"Take him away," I said to the guards.

I didn't give a damn about Mark.

He wasn't going to talk.

He'd sooner die, which only confirmed that he wasn't a random guy and had been sent by someone.

And yet, all I could think about now was finding Natalia and explaining...

Except, there was nothing to explain and nothing to say.

I was a monster.

Why pretend otherwise?

She didn't have to like me, and if she was afraid of me, all the better. She was here to bear me heirs anyway, not for anything else.

CHAPTER 9

Natalia

I RACED DOWN THE HALLWAY, trying to get as far away from that damn room as possible. When I glanced over my shoulder, I couldn't see Gianluca, so I breathed out a sigh of relief.

I leaned against the wall and closed my eyes, taking a shuddery breath. Exploring the house had seemed like a good idea until I'd seen Gianluca punching that guy.

Yeah, I knew stuff like that happened. I knew that there were traitors and spies and people that needed to be interrogated for the safety of the whole family.

But what Gianluca had been doing was different.

It was the look on his face.

The coldness.

The lack of any emotion.

Only his eyes had something in them. Something strange.

Wicked.

He might've even enjoyed what he'd been doing. The rumors about him might be true after all.

I didn't know who the guy he'd been punching was or what he'd done, but there was something seriously wrong with Gianluca if he didn't feel anything at all.

Whenever my dad had gone out to fight someone and when he returned, he'd had that look in his eyes that said he knew he'd had to kill people, but he hadn't enjoyed it. The weight of taking a life had been evident in his eyes. He'd regretted it, even if he hadn't had a choice.

But Gianluca...

I shuddered.

How was I supposed to have children with a man like that? When we'd had sex, he'd seemed sort of nice and caring.

But what if that had only been because he was trying

to manipulate me and get me to let my guard down around him? What if he'd simply been in a good mood?

I didn't want my son or daughter to suffer his wrath when things didn't go his way. Everyone expected me to give him a son. If I failed, what would happen to my daughter?

Would he hate her? Would he hurt her?

Who was he even? What was he truly like? Was he a coldhearted monster like people had said he was?

A door not too far away from me opened, and one of the maids rushed out.

"I'm coming! I'm coming!" she said, holding her phone or whatever it was between her shoulder and her ear while she collected her long blonde hair into a ponytail. "You know how much I hate blood."

I pressed myself flatter against the wall so she wouldn't see me. She was probably on her way to clean up the mess Gianluca had made, and if he asked her if she'd seen me, I didn't want her to tell him where I was.

I didn't want to see him.

Not until I had a plan.

I couldn't get pregnant. Not yet, at least. Not until I knew him better and I could make sure my children would be safe.

Hopefully, that hadn't already happened.

But what could I do? Just tell him no?

Only, he'd return me to my family then and our deal

would be over, which would mean all this had been for nothing.

I bit down on my lip. My gaze landed on the door through which the maid had come out.

Was that her room?

I pushed myself off the wall and glanced right and left. The hallway was still empty and I rushed to the door. When I tried the handle, the door slid open.

I stepped inside, my heart thudding loudly in my chest.

There was a huge chance this was going to go terribly wrong if I got caught in here, but I was new here, so I could say I'd gotten lost. The house was huge, so it wouldn't be all that unbelievable.

Maybe I could become friends with the maid if I figured out what she liked. Then I could ask her to bring me some birth control pills and not tell anyone. Except, that was probably going to take me too long.

Unfortunately, the room was small and plain. I couldn't see anything personal that could help me get the maid on my side.

Maybe she hated cleaning up blood, but I couldn't help her with that myself because everyone would see me and wonder what the hell was wrong with me.

I headed to a cabinet and opened a drawer. I rummaged through the things, even though I felt guilty about it. But it was just clothes.

I opened another drawer.

More clothes.

My hand collided with something that wasn't as soft as a shirt. I closed my fingers around it and pulled it out.

A box of birth control pills.

I let out a surprised gasp because I couldn't believe I'd just gotten this lucky.

"Hey! What are you—" The door burst open and the maid narrowed her gaze at me, but then shock and surprise filled her blue eyes. "Sorry, Mrs. Cavallaro. I didn't expect you here. I thought it was someone else."

I turned toward her, the box still in my hand.

Her eyes flew wide open. "I can explain! It's not what you think!"

I watched her for a few moments, wondering why she was suddenly scared. Surely, she wouldn't have to explain to her boss that she was taking birth control pills.

Unless...

The maid's shoulders were rigid, and her mouth opened and closed as if she was panicking about something.

Something that was forbidden and related to the pills in some way.

Wait, was she having sex with a guard? Because that was a no-no and super distracting as they were supposed to be working. At least at my house, so maybe it was the same here.

"Oh, I know everything. You don't have to say a thing." I lifted my chin up. "I saw it, and I have proof."

I had no idea if this was going to work, but the maid was freaking out for a reason. Even if I didn't know it for sure, it might still work.

"I'm going to tell my husband," I said, starting for the door.

"No! Please!" She got in my way, her hands clasped in front of her. "Cole was off duty. I swear! We didn't... Just please don't tell my boss. Please. I need this job, and if Cole gets sent somewhere I'm never going to see him again and I... I love him. Please."

The corners of her eyes were filled with tears.

"All right," I said. "I won't say anything, but I'm keeping this." I lifted the box. "And you won't tell anyone anything about it either."

Maybe I should've kept quiet about it, and she wouldn't have even noticed I'd taken it with me, but I didn't want her to accidentally mention it to anyone.

One word to someone, and rumors could easily spread and get to Gianluca.

"But..." Her brow furrowed.

"If you don't want to lose Cole, then you'll keep quiet." I didn't think one box of pills would be enough either.

Sure, Gianluca would wonder what was wrong, but he wouldn't be too suspicious until a few months passed.

I'd caught a glimpse of the monster he could be, and I wasn't sure what I was going to do just yet. But buying myself some time was good. Something could happen to Gianluca in the meantime, or my family might figure out a way to protect themselves.

Time.

It was all I needed. Just a little more time, even if I wasn't entirely sure if that would do me any good.

Yes, I was probably stalling because, deep down, I was terrified of becoming a mother. Terrified that I'd mess things up and wouldn't be able to protect my child.

Terrified of having a family with a stranger, even if that was supposed to be normal for people like me.

"Just think about it," I added. "If I get pregnant, I'll need more protection or more staff. Maybe I'll be taken away somewhere. Cole might go with me, and you'll have to stay here. It's best if things continue like they are for now. Don't you agree?"

I couldn't be a hundred percent sure Cole was a guard. Maybe his job was something else, but judging by the look in the maid's eyes, my story made sense to her.

"Yes, ma'am," she said.

"Good. Then we have a deal." I offered her a small smile. "What's your name?"

"Eve."

"All right, Eve. I hope Cole and you will be more careful in the future."

"Yes, ma'am."

I strode past her, hugging the box to myself. My heart was racing again as I hurried to my room before anyone saw me.

Once I was inside, I closed the door and leaned against it, letting out a sigh.

The box I held in my arms was now everything to me.

I dashed across the room and opened my closet, trying to find a good hiding spot. Before I stuffed the box under a pile of things, I took a pill into my hand.

After I made sure everything was in order, I shut the closet door and headed to the bathroom. I popped the pill into my mouth and got some water. As I swallowed, I looked at my reflection in the mirror.

What the hell was I doing?

Adelina would yell at me if she knew what I'd just done. She'd say I was fighting who I was for no reason and putting my whole family at risk.

She'd say that there was no reason to be afraid of anything, and that Gianluca would take care of his children because that was his duty.

But my sister wasn't here.

And I felt so damn alone. Eve so wasn't going to be my friend after I just blackmailed her.

My phone buzzed on the nightstand where I'd left it, making me jump. I hurried to pick it up.

There was a message from Gianluca, and my insides constricted.

What if Eve had told him something anyway? What if the house was bugged so he could always know what was going on around here?

But I supposed he wouldn't be texting me about it then.

I opened the message.

A gasp escaped my throat.

He wanted me to come to his room.

For sex.

If you want the same thing as last night, don't wear your panties.

If you want this...

There was a video.

I tapped the play button.

A jolt of heat shot through me.

Oh hell.

Why did these things have such an effect on me, especially when I was imagining Gianluca doing them?

How did that make any sense? Why did I want him?

No, I didn't want *him*.

I wanted pleasure.

I wanted to feel good.

No matter how crazy that sounded.

He'd let me have a taste, and I wanted more.

I looked down my dress. I needed to change, so I

raced to my closet to find something less plain. Once I grabbed a red cocktail dress, I reached for matching underwear.

I didn't think I needed a bra, but...

Panties or no panties?

What we'd done last night had been amazing, but...

Did I want to try something new? Would he hurt me?

I wanted to tell myself that I was doing this just because I wanted to test Gianluca. If he hurt me, I didn't think I'd ever want my child around him. And if he didn't, then maybe there was still hope.

But that was all bullshit because I was just so damn turned on.

Panties. Definitely panties.

When I was dressed, I took a deep breath as I glanced at my reflection in the mirror.

I got out into the hallway.

Gianluca's room was supposed to be on the other end of the house and it had to be a big one. Since he'd messaged me about sex, then I doubted we'd be talking about what I'd seen today, and I didn't want to think about it either.

The door to his room was cracked open, so I pushed it and entered.

A huge bed with dark covers occupied most of the space.

Gianluca grabbed my arm, making me yelp as he

yanked me to him. He nudged the door closed with his foot as his hands roamed my body.

I was already hot all over. He was only wearing a pair of black briefs, and his erection poked into me.

His hand trailed up my thigh and slipped under my dress. I let out a soft moan as his fingers grazed my panties.

"Good choice," he whispered into my ear, his lips brushing my earlobe, as he rubbed me through the fabric.

I leaned into his touch, forgetting about everything else.

Letting myself just feel.

He pulled away from me, and before I could see what he was doing, he caught my wrists. He must've grabbed a scarf or something from somewhere because he tied my wrists together behind my back.

A thrill surged through me.

When he got another scarf and started toward me, I backed away.

"That wasn't in the vid—"

"No, but I thought you might like it. If you don't, all you have to do is tell me."

"Okay. Fine." I let him place the scarf over my eyes and tie it behind my head.

I couldn't see anything.

I couldn't see him or what he was doing.

It should be scary, but it wasn't.

It was hot.

Gianluca didn't touch me. Actually, he was so quiet and didn't move at all that I had no idea what was going on.

Was he watching me?

Was he even here?

But I would've heard him leave, wouldn't I?

His fingers brushed my neck and then buried in my hair, forcing my head to the side. His mouth lowered to my exposed skin as he slid the strap of my dress down my shoulder.

A moan stole its way out of my throat as he kept kissing me and then tugged on my dress so hard that I heard it rip.

The torn fabric fell down, giving him access to my breasts. He pinched my nipples and toyed with my breasts, eliciting a groan of pleasure from me.

He ran his finger over my lips, pushing inside my mouth.

I let out a small cry when he grabbed my arm and shoved me down so I was bent over a hard surface, probably a desk.

He lifted my dress up, running his hands up and down my thighs and ass. His fingers caught the waistband of my panties and yanked down.

My insides tingled as he brought his palm hard on my bottom.

One smack.

Another.

And another.

I gasped at the delicious sting that spread through my heated flesh as he spanked me.

"Your ass should be red all the time. Looks so good," he said before a torrent of quick smacks landed on my sit spot.

I groaned, my pussy already dripping wet.

He rubbed my sore cheeks, and then his fingers slipped to my opening. I spread my legs wider as his fingers slid up and down my slit.

Pushing past my folds, his finger glided to my throbbing clit. His finger traced gentle circles over my bud, pressing and probing.

He still played with my clit, tormenting me and pushing me closer to the edge, as one of his fingers dipped inside me.

I moaned as another of his fingers pumped in and out of me, the pressure inside me impossible to contain.

I spilled over the edge with a cry, coming all over his fingers. He let go of me and didn't give me a chance to recover.

Just a moment after I felt his cock grazing me, he slammed himself inside me, all the way in. My arousal was back stronger than ever as he rocked his hips faster and faster.

He gripped my tied wrists as his forceful thrusts shook my whole body.

I couldn't keep quiet, even though I was afraid the whole house would hear me, as he pounded into me, his hold on me tightening.

When my pleasure rolled through me, it knocked my breath out of me. I gasped for air as my whole body throbbed and tingled.

Gianluca rammed himself into me again with a grunt, and then pressed himself against me as his cock pulsated inside me.

It seemed like we were suspended in time. Like we were someone else and not us.

Because if we were who we were, I couldn't understand how possibly this could feel so good or why I'd even enjoy doing this with him.

When Gianluca pulled away from me, and released my blindfold and untied my hands. I turned to him.

I didn't know what I was expecting to find on his face or in his eyes, but before I could see any of it, he spun and strode to the bathroom.

I let out a sigh.

Why did it again feel like I was being dismissed?

Like this whole thing at the end ruined everything we'd done before? Why did it bother me?

I'd gotten the pleasure that I'd wanted. I didn't feel anything for him, and it shouldn't upset me that he was cold to me later.

And yet, I wondered why. The guy who'd kissed my neck and touched me with so much passion couldn't be the same guy as the one who didn't feel anything for anyone.

Or could he?

Maybe it was just me who didn't quite understand how sex worked yet. People had sex and enjoyed themselves without needing something more all the time.

I was just being weird.

I pulled on my panties, fixed my dress as much as I could because some of it was torn, and then I stormed out of Gianluca's room.

CHAPTER 10

Gianluca

FUCKING MY WIFE JUST might turn into one of my favorite pastimes, and I couldn't stop thinking about her. Despite the cold shower, my body was still hot and ready for action.

Ready for her.

I didn't know what it was about her, but she'd pleasantly surprised me.

My phone rang, and I tossed away the towel that I'd used to dry myself off. As soon as I picked up the phone, I furrowed my brow.

My father's number was on the screen.

I answered.

"Gianluca," my father said. "I want you to take care of the Vinicellis for me. Someone needs to put them in their place and quickly."

A smile spread across my lips. "I thought you'd never ask."

"Call me when it's done."

The line went dead.

I texted Sebastiano and quickly got dressed. My hair was still damp when I got out into the hallway, but I didn't care.

It was finally happening.

I'd show my father he'd made a mistake when he'd trusted Bruno to do the job right. This was a job for me, and not for my brother.

Sebastiano was waiting for me outside, and all the men were already in their cars.

"Everyone's ready," he said.

"Perfect."

"What's the plan?"

"We'll do the one I've come up with ages ago. It'll still work. We'll leave the cars farther away and sneak up on the Vinicellis. We'll kill as many of them as we can in the dark, and they won't even know what happened to them."

"All right," Sebastiano said.

"Let's go." I wasn't about to waste a second because I could already taste my win.

I HELD UP MY GUN, WAITING to give my men a signal to start the attack. The Vinicelli men weren't suspecting anything, and we'd gotten all the way to their stash house unseen.

But, unlike my brother, I'd been monitoring this area for months, and it hadn't been easy to find the Vinicellis' hideout.

Just as I was about to lift my hand, shots rang out. The Vinicellis shouted and ran for cover.

Fuck!

I looked in Sebastiano's direction and wished I could see the look in his eyes, but it was too dark.

What the fuck had happened? Had the Vinicellis started a fight among themselves?

Had one of my men gotten trigger-happy too soon?

Except my men weren't that incompetent, or they wouldn't be with me here.

So what the fuck?

More shots rang out, and the Vinicellis were getting deeper and deeper into their holes. Finding them now might not be a problem, but they'd see us coming and they'd defend themselves.

Shit!

We'd have to try some other time, and not here.

Instead of sending them to attack, I signaled to my men to pull back.

Gritting my teeth, I couldn't stop thinking about what could've possibly happened.

Until I saw a red Ferrari whizzing away.

Son of a bitch!

Bruno.

He'd sabotaged my attack, hadn't he?

He must have. Somehow, he'd known I'd attack, and he'd fired those shots to warn the Vinicellis.

Was he working with them? Or was he only trying to fuck up my plan?

The answer was obvious.

It was the latter.

I broke into a run. If Bruno thought he was going to get away with this, he was wrong. As soon as I got to my car, I hopped in and gunned the engine.

I had an idea about where Bruno might be going, so I sped after him.

Just as I'd expected, the red Ferrari was parked right in front of Bruno's favorite house. But as I pulled over, I clenched the steering wheel so tightly my knuckles were white.

My father was here too.

Had he sent Bruno to sabotage me?

I got out of the car. My father's and Bruno's guards watched me as I strode to the front door. I almost kicked it open as I barged inside.

"What the fuck was that?" I went straight for Bruno. "Why the fuck did you do that?"

"Because I had to." Bruno glared at me.

I swung at him, getting him in the jaw.

He tried to punch me, but I evaded.

"Enough!" my father yelled. "Gianluca! Stop!"

"Are you still going to defend him?" I turned to my father, my blood racing. "I had it all planned to take care of the Vinicellis, and he," I pointed at my brother, "fucked it all up!"

"All Bruno wanted was to make sure you didn't fail. He saw a flaw in your plan, but it was too late to stop you, so he had to do what he had to do," my father said calmly.

"Do you really believe that pile of bullshit?" I snorted. "Of course you do. But there was no flaw. Bruno stopped me because he couldn't handle the fact that I'd succeed, unlike him!"

My brother glared at me, but he didn't say anything.

"Go home, Gianluca," my father said. "We'll talk about this some other time."

I caught myself reaching for my gun.

If Bruno were dead, this would be a whole lot easier.

But killing my brother and father went against everything I believed in, unless they attacked me first and I had no choice. That would be nowhere near as satisfying as beating Bruno at his own game.

I took a deep breath and slowly released it.

I met my father's gaze. "You know Bruno couldn't have known my whole plan, only what his spies had told him. If he'd wanted to help me, he would've called me and told me his concerns. Maybe you should ask him why he's so interested in having the Vinicellis think they have a chance against us."

Without another word, I spun around and stormed out of there.

My father was going to beg me for forgiveness one day.

I didn't know when it would happen, but that day was going to come, and then there would be no going back.

AS SOON AS I PARKED in my driveway, I got out of the car, ready to punch something. We always had someone in the dungeon, so there were plenty of candidates.

I didn't give a fuck what they'd done.

I needed the anger and tension racing through me to go somewhere else.

But as I opened the door and entered the foyer, I stopped dead in my tracks.

Natalia turned around.

Her gaze met mine, widening slightly. "Sorry. I know I'm not supposed to do this without asking first, but I thought—"

I stared around the foyer. The walls had always been empty here, but now there were paintings on them.

A plant was in the corner, and a vase with flowers on the small table that hadn't been used for years and had only been collecting dust.

The whole foyer was suddenly full of life, or maybe it was just Natalia.

"I like it," I said.

Her eyebrows shot up. "You do? So I don't have to take it all back?"

"No, of course not. This is your home too."

Why the fuck would my wife need to ask me permission to put a plant somewhere? I wasn't allergic to any plants.

Judging by the surprised look on Natalia's face, someone else must've objected when she'd tried to change things up, probably her family.

My stomach rumbled. Whatever anger I'd been feeling when I'd been on my way here had vanished somewhere.

Natalia had distracted me, and I didn't know how she'd pulled that off without even knowing it.

Things around here were always the same, and she was like a breath of fresh air. Enough to pull me out of my monotonous routine.

"Are you hungry?" I asked.

"A little." She shrugged. "But it's getting really late, and—"

"Doesn't matter. Come." I should be plotting revenge to make my brother pay for what he'd done, but there'd be time for that.

It could wait.

CHAPTER 11

Natalia

THE STAFF IMMEDIATELY prepared some sandwiches for Gianluca and me, and when everyone was gone, it was just my husband and I sitting at the table.

The sandwiches were delicious, but nothing could distract me from the tension in Gianluca's shoulders, although he didn't look as furious as he'd seemed the moment he'd entered the house.

"Is something wrong?" I asked.

He shook his head. "What you did in the foyer is amazing. Do you like to do that?"

I shrugged. "I've always enjoyed decorating and rearranging things. I think that many times our living space can be improved by even the smallest change."

"Why do I have a feeling someone didn't approve of your hobby?"

"Well, it's not really a hobby. I mean, my mom always wants everything to be exactly like she thinks my dad would like. Whenever I changed something, she'd be angry and put everything back the way it was. When I was very young, I found some paint and drew flowers on the wall of my room with it." A small smile tugged at the corners of my lips. "She completely lost it and called someone to paint my wall white again."

"Why?" His brow furrowed. "If you want to change something, change it. As long as you don't throw away or discard anything important that someone else might need, why would it matter, especially if it's your own room? Actually, if you want more stuff for your room, you can order it online and someone will bring it here safely."

"Really?" I gaped at him.

"Yeah. A lot of rooms in this house are empty, and no

one has the time or will to do anything about it, so if you want, just do it."

"And if you hate what I do?"

"I doubt that will happen, but if it does, it's easy to change things back or do something else."

I eyed him carefully. The corners of his lips were slightly upturned, and he was more relaxed.

Maybe there was something else I could ask if he was in a good mood again.

"I'd like to go see my family if that's not a problem," I said.

He pressed his lips into a tight line, his eyes narrowed at me.

I had a sensation I'd just said the wrong thing.

"Why?" He cocked his head.

"Um, what do you mean?"

He took a bite of his sandwich. "We've just gotten married, and you already want to run to your family. Have they tasked you with spying on me? Are they up to something? Maybe there's a reason why my brother refused to marry you."

"I don't know what you're talking about."

His shoulders were rigid again, and his frown deepened when he mentioned his brother. Something must've happened with his brother, but I had no idea what it was.

"You don't, huh? If you and your family aren't

plotting something with Bruno, then what other reason could you possibly have?" His eyes were hard on mine.

"I just wanted to see my family. That's all. I'm used to always having them with me, so I miss them. But I understand if that's not possible." I hoped we could change the subject because Bruno had to be the reason why Gianluca was so on edge.

"Is there someone else?" he asked. "Do you have a secret boyfriend you want to run off to now that you no longer have to be a virgin? Are you in love with someone?"

"What?" My mouth went slack. "I don't know how I could possibly do something like that when your guards would be with me all the time."

He let out a laugh. "Your mother found a way."

"You have no right to talk about my mom like that!" I raised my voice.

"Didn't she tell you? She was meeting with some guy until your father found out and killed him. Maybe that's why she didn't dare to go against your father, even when it came to decoration." He flashed me a smile that didn't reach his eyes.

"You're lying!" I got to my feet, nearly toppling over the chair.

Why was he saying all that? Just to hurt me? Hurt me because he was upset because of Bruno?

I'd almost lowered my guard around him.

Almost.

"I'm sure I still have the photos of her and the guy somewhere. I was tasked with watching them when I was fifteen. Your father covered everything up, of course. He didn't want everyone to laugh at him and humiliate him. And who knows? Maybe you're the one who's lying. Maybe mommy dearest told you everything about how to get the guards to look the other way so you can meet with the love of your life."

"I'm not lying, and I don't know what's wrong with you that you're coming up with all—" I paused, frowning at him. "Do *you* have someone? Is that it? You haven't lived your life sheltered from the whole damn world. Are you in love with someone? Are you hoping I'll do something wrong so you can get rid of me and bring her here?"

"In love? No, I'm not stupid enough to believe that shit exists, especially when it comes to us. People get together for various reasons, but love isn't it."

"Well, I agree with that, so stop accusing me of things that aren't going to happen."

No one I knew had gotten married for love, and I didn't think it would ever happen. My dad and my mom cared about each other, but I didn't think they truly loved each other, especially if what Gianluca had said was true.

I'd always thought that what bound them together was duty, family, and respect. Now, who knew?

"All right, but you're not leaving this house," Gianluca said, his face serious.

"So you're going to keep me your prisoner forever?"

"Only until you get pregnant and give me a son."

"You know what? I think you're mad about your brother, and you're taking it out on me. We'll talk some other time." I strode to the door.

My mom and my sister would've never done such a thing, but I wasn't about to wait for him to tell me I could leave.

I was done talking to him.

He didn't follow me or yell at me to come back.

Once I reached my room, I plopped down on the bed and groaned.

At least I didn't have to see Gianluca today anymore.

I GLANCED AT THE PHONE on my nightstand. Maybe I couldn't see my sister, but I could call her. I'd been tossing and turning in bed all night, and now I didn't feel like getting up.

I reached out for the phone, but then I hesitated. If I told my sister about what had happened yesterday, she'd probably tell me I'd done it all wrong.

She'd say that no matter how angry I was at my husband, I shouldn't let it show, and that I should've found a way to manipulate him to get what I wanted.

Get him to feel like he was in charge and making all the decisions while I was nudging him in that direction from the start.

Only, most of the time that made absolutely no sense to me.

Why should I ask my husband permission to go see my family? All I should be asking was if it was safe for me to do that since he knew best what was up in the mafia world.

Nothing else.

I snatched the phone and found my sister's number.

"Hi, it's Natalia. I'd like to talk to my sister," I said as one of Enrico's staff answered.

She never ever answered the phone herself, so I was pretty sure all the staff knew the sound of my voice. Besides, not just anyone would have this number.

"I'm sorry, ma'am," the woman on the other side of the line said. "Mrs. Pagani isn't available right now."

"Do you know when she *will* be available?"

"No, ma'am."

"Right. Thanks." I ended the call.

Enrico didn't want Adelina to talk to me.

I had no idea what he was afraid of. Maybe that we'd share some weird family secrets, which didn't make any sense because everyone monitored all the calls, so saying anything weird would be super risky.

I stared at the phone.

My mom would answer if I called, but could I ask her if what Gianluca had told me was true?

I really wanted to know, especially if she'd actually been in love with that guy, but talking about that was a terrible idea and I didn't want to bring up bad memories.

Maybe there'd be a time for that conversation, but it definitely wasn't now.

WHEN THE NIGHT FELL, I fought the urge to turn off my phone. But Gianluca didn't have to text me. He could just come to my room.

As I lay on the pillows, I wasn't sure what to think.

After our conversation, having sex with him as if nothing had happened would be weird.

Yeah, I'd been able to tune out the rest of my thoughts when I was with him and when he touched me with his expert fingers, but I doubted I could do that today.

I was confused about him more than ever. The sex was amazing, but maybe that was only because he was my first and only.

I shouldn't just be looking forward to sex.

He could be nice, though.

He'd shown me that, but it had been too short of a glimpse.

Just because he'd allowed me to change some things around the house couldn't erase and make me forget everything else he'd said to me and that I'd seen him do.

But a few days was nowhere near enough to really get to know someone.

I heard footsteps in the hallway, and my heart skipped a beat.

They were coming closer, and closer, and closer.

CHAPTER 12

Gianluca

I STOOD IN FRONT OF the door to Natalia's room.

She'd been right yesterday when she'd said I'd been mad about something else. I didn't know why I'd told her all those things.

It was all Bruno's fault.

He'd pissed me off, as usual, and even though

Natalia had chased away some of my fury, she couldn't erase it.

It wasn't her fault my relationship with my brother—and the rest of my family—was fucked up.

I couldn't understand why anyone would want to be around their family when they didn't have to, but she might not agree with me on that.

At least she and I had something in common. We didn't believe in love, which should make our marriage simpler.

Even though I needed her to get pregnant sooner rather than later, I didn't want sex to become a chore.

With a sigh, I strode down the hallway and to my own room.

I needed to clear my head, so I headed to the bathroom to take a cold shower.

But once I stood under the freezing water, my thoughts kept flying to Natalia.

My hand slid down to my cock.

I pictured spreading Natalia's legs and diving deep, deep inside her, making her take me all in.

I pictured her rising breasts and her moans.

I stroked myself until I came, but even then, I could still see her in my mind.

The way she'd glared at me with so much fire in her eyes.

Fire she rarely allowed herself to let out.

Even when she was furious, she was holding back.

Why was it so hard for her to set herself free?

She's a mafia princess, you idiot.

She's not a free woman.

She's never been free, not truly.

I curled my fingers into a fist and slammed my hand against the wall.

Instead of thinking about Natalia, I should be planning something to do about my brother. I didn't believe the Bonamontes and Bruno had some kind of deal and that Natalia was part of it.

But Bruno was definitely up to something.

He'd failed to take care of the Vinicellis, and then he'd sabotaged me so I wouldn't succeed either. I'd think he was trying to impress Father, but he would've agreed to get married if he wanted that.

So what was his deal now?

It was still a mystery.

Unless he'd changed his mind after I stole Natalia from him.

I let the cold water drip down my body, even if it wasn't helping with clearing my mind.

My phone, which I'd left on the sink, buzzed.

I turned off the shower and wiped my hands on a towel.

When I checked my phone, a text from my father was on the screen.

He wanted me to come to a family dinner.
Huh.
Was that a trap?
Or an opportunity?

CHAPTER 13

Natalia

GIANLUCA'S FINGERS traced a path up my thigh. He shoved my legs apart, lowering his mouth to my center.

Heat filled my insides, and I waved my hand, trying to find something to hold onto as his tongue swirled over my clit.

A loud thud made me open my eyes.

Shit!

A dream.

It had been a dream, and I'd managed to send my phone flying to the floor.

This was what I got for falling asleep while thinking about Gianluca, or rather, about having sex with Gianluca.

I had no idea what was wrong with me.

As I fished the phone off the floor, I was glad to see it hadn't broken. Even the screen was still intact.

As I tapped it, I noticed I had a message.

It was from Gianluca.

He and I were supposed to go to a family dinner later today, and he had some business to do, so he'd just come pick me up later.

Huh.

Should I be glad that he hadn't come to me last night? Or worried?

Oh, and let's ignore that part of me that has to be some kind of sex addict.

But dinner sounded good. Maybe I'd finally find out more about Gianluca and figure out what was up with him and his brother.

I dialed my sister's number.

It was still early in the morning, so maybe Enrico was busy somewhere and wouldn't have the time to forbid her from receiving my calls.

"Hi. It's Natalia. Can I—"

"Yes, ma'am."

Ha! Finally some luck.

"Nat?" Adelina said. "What's up? I've been dying to hear from you."

"I tried to call you, but they told me you weren't available."

She sighed. "I know. Enrico wanted me with him all the time, but it doesn't matter. Tell me everything!"

"There's not much to tell. Everything's fine, except... I asked Gianluca to let me see my family—I really miss Mom, Dad, and Ciro and Gabriel—but he was mad about something else and he snapped at me. He said I wouldn't be allowed out of the house until I gave birth to his son or something like that. I hope he'll forget all about it."

"He will. Just find out what he likes and do it for him. If he's happy, he's more likely to agree to whatever you want him to agree."

"But that's so stupid! I should be able to see my family whenever the hell I want. I'm not his prisoner. I'm his wife."

"It's not that simple."

"Why don't we make it simple?"

"I have everything I've ever wanted with Enrico. I can buy whatever I want. He's making that possible for me. I'm not hungry or cold, and I don't have to go out there somewhere to smuggle drugs or shoot people, or whatever it is that he has to do. And he promised to take me on a trip when he goes on a vacation. So what if I can't always go out when I want to and if I have to do some things to please him? Just enjoy what you have and don't think about what you don't. Unless it can be bought."

I made a face.

Why couldn't I be happy about it like she was? Instead, my stomach flipped upside down just thinking about it.

Actually, the more I thought about it, the more disgusting it seemed. And why wouldn't I want to be part of the business?

Maybe not torturing and killing people, but not everyone did that. The mafia wasn't just about drugs, weapons, and killing.

There were so many things I could do, but someone at some point had decided it wasn't allowed, and now everyone was running with it even to this day, probably because it benefited them.

"Oh, I have some tips that could help you get pregnant quicker that I found in a magazine," Adelina said.

My gaze fell on my closet. It was time to take another pill. I so didn't want to hear anything about pregnancy right now.

If my sister could see what I was doing, she'd hit me over the head, and she wasn't even a violent person.

"Are you writing this down?" she asked.

"Yes, sure. Thank you so much." I had no idea what she'd said because I'd tuned it all out.

"I gotta go. Call me sometime, and I'm sure you'll convince Gianluca to let you see us all. Bye!"

"I hope so. Bye." I let out a sigh.

Maybe I could actually take some of my sister's advice. She'd mentioned I should find out what Gianluca liked. Maybe there was a way to do that, especially when I knew that he was away.

I quickly drank my pill and got ready, and then I headed to Gianluca's room.

The last time I'd been there... Well, I'd been distracted and blindfolded.

I tried the handle and the door opened. As I entered, my gaze fell on the desk over which Gianluca had fucked me.

A shot of heat zapped through me.

Damn.

I forced my gaze away from the desk.

Something he likes.

Find something he likes.

The only problem was that the room was plain and boring. Sure, the furniture was amazing, and the tech too, but it was all too clean and too perfect.

I wasn't sure if there was something Gianluca really liked or if all that stuff was just in his room because someone had thought it should be there.

I traced my finger over the stack of old video games and came away with dust. Maybe he'd played those ages ago, but not now.

The first drawer I opened was full of clothes.

Another with weapons, and I almost reached out for a gun just to see how it would feel in my hand. Despite literally being surrounded by weapons at all times, no one had ever allowed me to even touch one.

I closed the drawer so I wouldn't get tempted and headed to the closet. When I opened it, I spotted a box. Carefully pulling it out, I took a peek inside.

A basketball.

Huh. Maybe that was something old too, even though it was in perfect condition and looking almost brand new.

I returned the box. At the bottom of the closet, I found a stack of papers.

Sketches.

My eyebrows shot up.

They were really good.

Cars.

Girls.

Guns.

And... Um, sex.

I tilted one of the sketches, unsure from which angle I was supposed to look at it. It was some weird sex pose, or maybe it was just weird to me.

Had Gianluca sketched all that? If he had, he was really talented, but the sketches looked old too.

Had the mafia completely taken over his life once he'd grown up?

So much that he no longer had any time for the things he liked?

Or did he believe enjoying those things wasn't appropriate for a future mafia boss?

My shoulders slumped as I sighed. The whole thing seemed so sad. But should I feel sorry for Gianluca or not?

I put everything back where it belonged and shut the closet.

If I wanted to figure out if there was still something Gianluca liked, I wouldn't find it here. That was obvious now, so I headed back to my room.

I HAD TO GET READY for the Cavallaros' dinner, and I had no idea what to wear.

Adelina and my mom would suggest something sexy—something that would catch everyone's attention and show everyone just how lucky the husband was.

Unless, of course, said husband objected for some reason.

Gianluca hadn't given me any suggestions or anything, so I supposed I was free to choose.

But since it was a family dinner, it was better to choose something that would keep people's eyes off me. I didn't want to be the center of attention.

I searched through my clothes and finally found what I needed. It was a black turtleneck dress with long sleeves. Boring and perfect for the occasion.

I'd just sit there with Gianluca and wait for the whole thing to end.

Invisible.

IT TURNED OUT I COULDN'T be invisible when I was Gianluca's wife.

As we were seated at the table, Gianluca's brother kept throwing glances at me, and his eyes were so intense that his gaze scared me, and I was glad I hadn't run into him in a dark alley—not that that would ever be possible since I always had guards with me, but still.

Gianluca's dad was openly staring at me too, but with a frown on his face. Since his wife was wearing a long blue gown with a big cleavage and a huge slit on the side, I was pretty sure he didn't like my dress.

Or he just didn't like me.

Whenever I met the gaze of Gianluca's mom, she looked away as if she was afraid to look anyone in the eye. There were also some people I didn't know, probably relatives.

"So, Gianluca," Franco said. "When is my grandson coming?"

"For fuck's sake, Father," Gianluca said. "It's only been a few days."

"I know. I know. But you mustn't forget your priorities." He glanced at me.

"How could I ever forget?" Gianluca's shoulders tensed. "You constantly keep reminding me."

"Do you remember when you were ten and you told me to stop reminding you not to let that gun out of your sight? We lost a valuable family heirloom because you left it somewhere. I don't know why I even let you touch it. I had so much faith in you, and look where—"

"What does that have to do with anything?" Gianluca's jaw was clenched.

"Let's hope it doesn't."

I stared at Franco, barely believing he'd just brought up a mistake from the time when Gianluca was only ten years old, in the middle of a family dinner. And it sounded like he was hinting that Gianluca might disappoint him again.

That was just terrible. Who the hell did that to their child?

I reached out for Gianluca's hand under the table.

When my fingers brushed his, he flinched. His surprised gaze met mine, and I covered his hand with mine. I expected him to pull away or look at me like I was crazy, but he didn't.

"When we're sharing such fond memories, why don't we talk about that time when I was six and Bruno tried to drown me in our pool?" Gianluca glanced at his brother.

"That was an accident," Franco said.

"Yeah, that's right. An accident. Like with the Vinicellis."

"Let's not talk business." Franco's lips spread into a smile. "Tonight is all about family." He actually tapped Bruno's shoulder.

Sure, they were sitting right next to each other, but Franco didn't even spare Gianluca a glance.

So much about family.

Gianluca's mouth was pressed tightly together as he glared at Bruno, who was staring right back at him with narrowed eyes.

Oookay, the Cavallaro family dynamics were something else.

Scary, even.

And Franco wasn't helping at all to heal the rift between his sons. He was actually adding fuel to the fire, and it almost seemed like he wanted Gianluca to fail, which was weird, considering Gianluca was also his son.

"Where's the bathroom?" I asked Gianluca, just to stop the staring contest between the brothers.

"Down the hallway, to the right."

I got to my feet, feeling Bruno's gaze on me.

No wonder Gianluca was angry a lot. His family was insane.

Once I got to the bathroom, I leaned on the sink and let out a sigh. Being around the Cavallaros was exhausting, and I really needed a break.

The door burst open, making me yelp.

Bruno strode toward me so fast I tried to back away but collided with the sink. He roughly caught me by the arm, tearing at my dress.

"Stop!" I yelled.

"Hey! Let go of her!" Gianluca tore Bruno off me, shoving him back.

I was still in shock, my heart racing, as Gianluca caught Bruno by the lapels of his shirt and punched him hard in the face.

"What is going on here?" Franco asked.

"He attacked my wife!" Gianluca yelled.

Bruno had stumbled back and was wiping blood off his face.

Franco got in Gianluca's way. "You know fighting is forbidden during dinner. Leave!"

"But he—You know what? Fuck you! All of you!" Gianluca grabbed my hand and pulled me with him.

I was glad to be out of there, so I didn't mind as he dragged me to the parking lot. The guards moved when they saw us, but Gianluca didn't wait for them.

"Get in the car," he said, and I did.

He brought the engine to life, and then we were speeding away.

Gianluca gripped the steering wheel, his face completely empty of all emotion. When the lights hit his eyes, I saw them swirling with emotion.

Why was he even still with his family if they treated him like that? Why hadn't he refused the invitation?

Getting out of the mafia or branching out on your own without the boss' blessing was hard, but wouldn't he prefer to avoid them as much as possible?

I wanted to ask, but I had to clutch my seatbelt because we were whizzing down the street so fast I thought I was going to be sick.

"Please slow down," I said, but Gianluca only smiled and stepped on the gas pedal even harder.

We zigzagged through the cars and even flew through a red light.

My chest heaved, bile rising at the back of my throat.

"Gianluca..." I whispered, but he didn't listen.

I let out a cry when a car came at us out of nowhere. My heart jumped into my throat.

Gianluca swerved at the last moment, barely avoiding collision.

I was shaking all over by the time he pulled over in our driveway. When I got out of the car, the ground was dancing in front of my eyes.

I took a deep breath, straightening my shoulders.

And then I strode to Gianluca, who'd just gotten out of the car, and I slapped him so hard that my palm stung.

CHAPTER 14

Gianluca

MY CHEEK STUNG AS I watched Natalia storm inside. The adrenaline was slowly fading from my system.

She was mad at me.

I remembered the moment she'd touched my hand under the table, trying to give me comfort. No one had ever done that for me.

And once again, I'd fucked things up with her.

I didn't want to feel bad about it, but I did.

A car pulled over next to mine. Sebastiano got out, his eyes narrowed at me, his lips tight with disapproval.

Yet another person I'd disappointed.

Fucking great.

"Where were you?" I flashed him a smile. "You're supposed to be my guard. My wife just assaulted me, and you weren't even here to stop her."

"You know full well you deserved it." Sebastiano's face was deadly serious, so I supposed my attempt at a joke had failed too. "Grow up, Gianluca. If you want to keep trying to kill yourself, I know I can't stop you. But at least have the decency not to drag anyone else down with you. You're not alone anymore. Don't forget that."

"I'm not trying to kill myself."

Sebastiano shook his head at me, and then he brushed past me and walked away.

I raked my hand through my hair.

Fuck.

I was never going to do or say the right thing, was I? It was like a curse that I didn't know how to break.

I COULDN'T SLEEP, SO I poured myself some whiskey and headed onto the terrace.

But I wasn't alone.

Natalia was there, and when she turned her head and saw me, she hugged herself.

As if she was scared of me.

And maybe she was.

I didn't like that at all.

She hurried to the door.

"Natalia, wait," I said.

She paused, turning to me.

"I'm sorry."

She tilted her head. "For what? For your brother attacking me in the bathroom? Or because you almost got us killed?"

"We're not dead," I said with a small smile.

She just glared at me.

"I shouldn't have put your life at risk. It's my duty to protect you, and I failed at that."

"Why do you do that to yourself?"

"Do what?" I had no clue what she was talking about.

"I may not know much about you, but your family is just... Why do you even still accept their invitations if they act like they did tonight? Or was tonight an exception?"

I wished it was. "It's not that simple. I'm a Cavallaro. My father is the boss. Everyone, including my men, ultimately belongs to him. If I try to leave and form something on my own, they'd all come for me. Another option is to kill my father and my brother, but I don't want to do that. It's not how things should go, and it's against my family code. It would create discord among the men, and everyone would think they can just kill the leader and take over." I took a gulp of my drink.

"Did your brother really try to drown you?" she asked, her eyes filled with compassion I didn't know what to do with.

"Yeah. He held my head under the water. If Sebastiano hadn't seen him and pulled him off me, he would've succeeded."

"And your father believed your brother's story?"

I nodded. "He always does. That's why I'm looking forward to seeing Bruno fail at everything. Then they both won't have a choice but to admit their defeat."

"What if your father keeps denying it all?"

"He can't deny it forever. His men will get antsy and

start questioning his sanity. They're all with him now, out of respect, but that can change. And I'll be waiting for my moment. It will come."

"Why did Bruno attack me?"

"I don't know. Did he say anything to you?"

She shook her head. "Even if he had, I don't think I would've heard him. I was in shock. Do you believe he wanted to hurt me?"

"I don't know, but I won't let him anywhere near you ever again. I should've known he was up to something when he got up after you."

"Does your father always side with Bruno?"

"Yeah."

She frowned. "Why?"

"That's a good question. I guess it's because he can't stand the idea of his firstborn not living up to his expectations, so he prefers to lie to himself."

"But why put you down then? Can't he be happy for you too?"

"I guess not."

"That's just weird. My parents can be happy for both my sister and me, even though Adelina is perfect and she's basically everything my parents were ever hoping for. Me..." She grimaced. "I'm trying, but I always feel like I'm disappointing them, even when they don't say anything about it."

"Why would you be disappointing them? You saved them when you agreed to marry me. That was your choice, right? They haven't forced you."

"Yeah, it was my choice. But I don't know. I just…" She shrugged. "I'll never be Adelina."

"Why would you want to be her? What's the thing you most want in life?"

"I want to serve my family as best as I can and make them proud."

"That's all?" I eyed her carefully. "That's all you would've wanted even if you hadn't married me?"

"Yeah."

She was lying.

She had to be.

There was a spark in her eyes when she was talking about something that mattered to her, like that time when she'd talked about painting walls and rearranging stuff.

But now there was none of that.

Was she saying what she thought I wanted to hear? My mother tended to do that with my father because she'd been raised to behave that way.

Or was my wife deluding herself because she was too scared, or because it was impossible for her to go for her real dreams?

I wanted to ask, but I doubted she'd tell me, or even know the answer.

I glanced down at my glass. It wasn't even empty yet, and I was perfectly calm. Talking to Natalia had done that.

There was just something about her.

That *something* I kept noticing and still wasn't sure what exactly it was.

"You should call your mother and your sister," I said.

"Why?" Her shoulders tensed.

"I assume your father is busy and your brothers are at school, so the four of us could go somewhere for coffee."

"Wait, you'd be coming with me?" She eyed me with suspicion.

"Yeah. I want to see why you think your sister's perfect, and then I want to see your face when you realize she's not."

"What?" Her mouth fell open, but then she laughed. "Really?"

"Yeah." I felt my lips spread into a smile too.

Natalia's effect on me was intriguing.

I wanted to explore it.

Figure it out.

I wanted to get to know her.

Really know her.

And I wanted to free her of her insecurities because I had a feeling her eyes would sparkle even more then.

It was all for selfish reasons, though. I wanted to

occupy my mind with something other than my family's bullshit.

Or at least that was what I told myself.

CHAPTER 15

Natalia

AS GIANLUCA AND I WERE on our way to meet with my mom and Adelina, I took a deep breath that did nothing to alleviate the heavy feeling in my stomach.

It was part excitement, part anxiety.

Gianluca might have joked that Adelina wasn't as

perfect as I thought she was, but I was sure she was going to find a way to charm him in a few seconds.

I shouldn't be thinking about that. It didn't matter anyway. The only thing that was important here was that I'd see my mom and my sister.

I missed them.

Gianluca parked the car not too far away from the cafe where we were supposed to meet my mom and Adelina. The guards were right behind us as we strolled toward the cafe.

Gianluca looked impossibly handsome in his black suit, and I was sure Adelina would think my green dress was too plain and not sexy enough.

"You look amazing," Gianluca said with a small smile on his face.

My eyebrows shot up.

Had he been reading my mind? Or had he just noticed the crease on my forehead as I'd looked down at my dress?

"Thanks," I said softly.

"I thought you were looking forward to seeing your family."

"I am. I'm just... I don't know. I love them, but sometimes they can be a little too much."

"Then don't let them become too much." He took my hand, his fingers intertwining with mine.

Easy for him to say, but my family was less messed

up than his. Or at least I hoped so.

I couldn't see my family through someone else's eyes, so who knew what Gianluca would think about them.

I steeled myself and then did my best to relax my shoulders. Nothing bad was going to happen.

I was overreacting and overthinking things like always.

Now all I had to do was let go.

"I WAS ALWAYS IMPRESSED with how fast she could run," Adelina said, smiling at Gianluca. "One second I was watching her, and I blinked, and she was gone."

Aaaand my family couldn't stop talking about me for some reason, probably because they thought they were helping to endear me to Gianluca or something. Or they simply didn't want to talk about other things in front of him.

"Yes," my mom chimed in. "We already had our guards looking for her. Found her climbing an apple tree."

"Okay, can we talk about something else now?" I was desperate for a change of subject.

"Why, honey?" my mom asked. "I'm sure Gianluca loves to hear more about you. Isn't that right?"

Unfortunately, Gianluca nodded.

"Oh, Mom," Adelina said. "Do you remember when Nat saw that lawyer in a TV show and she pretended to be her? She even said she wanted to become one."

"Yeah, I do. That was hilarious. A lawyer!" My mom burst into laughter, placing her hand over her stomach.

My sister laughed too and even had to wipe tears that had appeared in the corners of her eyes.

Well, I was glad they found that hilarious.

Not.

I kept my lips up in a forced smile.

Gianluca's eyes were on me. I waited for him to start laughing too.

A mafia princess who dreamed of being a lawyer. Ha ha. What a joke, right?

"I have some business I need to attend to," Gianluca suddenly said. "You should go shopping. There are some good stores in this area."

"Of course! That's a great idea!" my mom said.

"Do you have your phone?" Gianluca asked me as he got to his feet.

"Yeah."

Adelina grinned at me as if she thought I'd just won

the lottery.

"I'll see you later." Gianluca winked and walked away.

At least he wouldn't have to hear any other embarrassing stories about me.

"How much do you think you can spend?" Adelina reached across the table. "Give me your phone! I want to see!"

"No. Not now, please."

"Oh, come on." Adelina pouted. "You've totally won him over. Sitting here with us and then letting you go shopping with us! And so soon! Do you remember how long it took me to convince Enrico to—"

"Let's go." I rose to my feet.

The last thing I wanted now was to feel guilty that I wasn't grateful enough.

"You need a new dress," Adelina said, looking me up and down. "This one's awful."

"I agree," my mom said.

I fought the urge to roll my eyes. "How's Carlo? When will I get to see him?"

"He's wonderful," Adelina beamed. "I have some photos I can show you."

Of course, letting anyone really get close to the Pagani heir was unacceptable, even if I was his aunt.

"Look," Adelina said, showing me the screen of her phone. "He's adorable, isn't he?"

"He is." A small smile curved my lips.

"I'm so terrified he'll grow up too quickly."

"Why?" I frowned.

"Enrico wants to send him to some school as soon as possible. I think they accept kids as young as four."

"And you won't be able to go with him?"

She shook her head. "It's a really good private school. I don't want him to go, but it's not up to me."

"But you're his mom! Your opinion should matter too."

"Let's see what they have here." My mom grabbed my arm and tugged me into a store before Adelina or I could say anything else.

I strolled around the store, not seeing anything I liked too much. It would be easier to go to a regular store and then combine a few elements to get something exciting and new.

When I was little, my dad had let me buy a few cheap dresses, and with the help of a maid who worked at our house, I'd cut and sewn parts of the dresses to make a new, beautiful, and unique one.

If only I could go back to that time.

But then my family would call me childish, and maybe I was.

"You should try this one on," my mom said, handing me a purple dress with a deep V-neck.

I took the dress, staring at it. There was nothing

special about it, except the price tag. Were we buying tons of stuff in places like this one just to make ourselves feel better about our lives and to make our sacrifices seem worth the trouble?

Just so that we didn't think we were birds trapped in cages, even if our cage was made out of gold?

I lifted my gaze, my lips parting. A beautiful dark purple suit. I wondered how it would look on me, but Adelina and my mom would flip if they caught me even looking at it.

I glanced down at the dress that I was holding. It was very similar in color. If I snatched the suit and hid it under the dress, then maybe I could have my five minutes and satisfy my curiosity in the changing room.

Be a lawyer princess for a few moments, not a mafia princess.

Well, a mafia princess in a family like mine or Gianluca's. Maybe some other mafia princesses out there had different traditions and lives.

A smile tugged at my lips.

When my mom and Adelina weren't watching, I dashed forward and grabbed the suit.

"I'm going to try this one," I said, pointing at the dress.

"Okay, honey," my mom said, a pleased smile on her face.

Adelina gave me a thumbs-up.

I hurried to the changing room. Hopefully, my mom and Adelina would be too busy to notice anything odd was going on.

Once I took off my dress and put on the suit, I grinned at my reflection in the mirror. It fit me perfectly, and hell, it was even sexy because I was only wearing a bra under the jacket.

I pictured myself strolling down the street, free, without any guards around. For a moment, I was someone with a different life.

A completely different person.

But I knew that fantasy couldn't last long.

I was about to take the suit off when I heard the curtain swish open. My brain was already coming up with an excuse for either my mom or Adelina who must've come to see the dress, but then someone's arms wrapped around me.

I yelped.

"Shh," Gianluca said into my ear.

"How did you get in here?" I whispered.

"I have my ways."

I froze because his arms were still around me, and we were both looking at our reflection in the mirror.

Gianluca's hand slipped under the suit jacket and cupped my breast through my bra. I let out a groan as heat rushed through me.

"Don't close your eyes," he murmured as his hands

lowered down my stomach. "I want you to see your face when I make you come."

Another wave of heat surged through me as he unzipped my pants, yanking them down with my underwear.

I gasped, wondering if we should be doing this here, but I didn't want him to stop touching me either.

If someone heard me or came to check where I was, especially my mom or Adelina, I'd be mortified, but the danger of it all was making the whole thing even more exciting.

Gianluca's hand dipped between my legs, and I leaned on the wall while I stared at my reflection in the mirror.

I was dripping wet when Gianluca's fingers slid inside me. When his finger flicked over my clit, I choked back a moan.

The pressure inside me intensified as Gianluca kept rubbing me and teasing me, his fingers exploring my folds.

When I felt his thick length poking at me, every inch of me was on fire.

I couldn't take it anymore.

I needed him inside me.

Once he rammed himself inside me, I let out a small cry. Gianluca put his hand over my mouth as he pounded into me, his thrusts hard, deep, and punishing.

Small sounds of pleasure escaped my throat anyway as his hips slammed against mine, my peak getting closer and closer.

I met Gianluca's gaze in the mirror as he throbbed inside me. One more powerful thrust, and my body exploded with all kinds of sensations.

His hand clamped tighter over my mouth, muffling my moan as my release spread through me like a wave.

My knees almost gave out, but Gianluca's strong arm was around me and keeping me up.

When he moved his hand away from my mouth, he spun me around. His eyes met mine, and then he kissed me with all the passion in the world.

"Honey?" my mom called.

My eyes went wide.

Gianluca only smiled.

"I'll be right out," I yelled back.

"Okay, honey." Luckily, she didn't come any closer.

"I need to change," I whispered to Gianluca.

Was I going to hide him as if he were my secret lover or what?

"No, you don't," he said. "Put the suit back on. I like it."

"Really?" I arched an eyebrow at him as I grabbed my bag so I could find some wet wipes.

"Yeah." He took hold of the jacket and buttoned it up.

After I cleaned myself up and pulled the pants up, I

checked myself out in the mirror. Hopefully, there weren't any stains or anything on the suit.

"It's fine," Gianluca said. "Go."

I walked out of the changing room.

"What is that, honey?" my mom asked when she saw me, her brow creased. "Why are you wearing that? Take it off! Your husband won't—"

"Her husband loves it," Gianluca said behind my back.

"Oh, I didn't know you were here. I haven't seen you come in." My mom's face effortlessly turned up into a smile. "She looks lovely in anything she puts on, doesn't she?"

I inwardly groaned.

"She does." Gianluca wound his arm around me, and then he pulled off the tag.

As he went to pay for the suit, Adelina showed up with a silver dress in her hands. Her mouth tightened when she saw me and then Gianluca. But then she smiled at me.

"Nice," she said.

I glanced at Gianluca. His gaze met mine, and he gave me another smile.

Who the hell was this guy?

Definitely not the one who'd almost driven us to our deaths.

Or maybe he was.

I liked him way better when he wasn't angry.

"Hey, baby." I heard a familiar voice, so I turned to my sister.

Enrico was by her side.

"I didn't expect to see you here," Adelina said.

"I finished my meeting early. We're leaving."

"Oh, okay. Can I buy this first?" She lifted the dress to show him as a smile danced on her face.

He barely even looked at the dress. "No."

"Why not? It will only take a second."

"Because it's my money and I decide what I want you to wear. Now let's go." He snatched the dress, tossed it away, and grabbed her by the arm and pulled her with him.

"Bye!" She waved at my mom and me, her smile melting into a grimace as Enrico led her to the door.

He was hurting her.

"Are you okay?" Gianluca asked.

"Yeah."

Except, nothing seemed okay.

I wanted Enrico away from my sister. I wanted to be able to see my nephew, and I didn't want him or any child sent away to some private school when they were only four.

But I supposed no one really cared about what I wanted.

CHAPTER 16

Gianluca

EVER SINCE THE DAY we'd met with her family, Natalia had seemed off. She was often pensive, her brow furrowed, as if she was thinking hard about something.

But she never shared her thoughts with me, and why would she?

I was still intrigued by her, especially after she'd

chosen that suit. She really *did* look awesome in anything she put on—and even better when she was naked—but it was impossible to forget the hurt look on her face when her mother and sister had ridiculed her dreams.

Today, I had something special in mind. It had been ages since I'd been to a basketball game. It was a major headache for Sebastiano and my guards, but I didn't give a damn.

It might cheer Natalia up.

"Have you ever been to a game before?" I asked as we were on our way to our seats.

She shook her head. "Not really. My father would never allow it."

"Mine never approved either. He thinks it's an unnecessary risk and that we shouldn't expose ourselves like this, but I think it's safer than getting caught at a restaurant during a business meeting. Killing your enemy in here would catch all kinds of bad attention. All the cops would be after you, and with even more security, it would be an organizational nightmare."

We got to our seats.

Natalia's smile was genuine as she looked around. The guards were right there with us, but I didn't think they would spoil the enjoyment.

We could pretend we were normal people here.

"So would your father prefer if you brought a whole

basketball team to your back yard so they could play just for you?" Natalia flashed me a smile.

"No. He doesn't approve of anything that's fun."

"Oh."

"He thinks our lives should be completely focused on business and that nothing should distract us from it."

"I get that." Her smile faded. "My family thinks I should focus on looking pretty and having children. Nothing else should get in the way."

Her gaze flitted to mine, her shoulders tensing as if she thought she'd just said the wrong thing or too much.

I hated when she did that.

I hated when she lied and pretended everything was okay when it wasn't.

I didn't know why it bothered me so much.

"When you told me your dream was to serve your family, did you mean you wanted to be a lawyer so you could help with all the contracts and getting people out of jail?" I asked.

Her eyes bulged. "I... It was just a silly dream I had as a kid."

"Are you sure about that? If you were free to choose what you wanted to do, without worrying about your family, me, or anyone else, what would you do?"

She licked her lips, and I wondered if she was going to lie to me again. "I'd be going to law school, yes. And yes, I'd like to be able to help. To do something. Why would we have to focus all our energy only on one thing? Either family or business. Why not both? Why not just be with your kid instead of sending him to some fancy private school when he's so young? Why—Sorry, I'm still upset over something Adelina said and I—"

"No, don't be. It's not a silly dream. What did Adelina say?"

"Her husband wants to send my nephew to some private school as soon as he turns four. I mean, four. That's just insane. The boy should be with his parents. I can't picture him so small and alone in some cold room." Her eyes teared up.

I caught her hand in mine, squeezing gently. I'd never even thought about any of that or about what I'd do once I had a child.

My phone buzzed in my pocket, and I pulled it out with my other hand.

My father's number flashed on the screen and I swore under my breath.

"Is something wrong?" Natalia asked.

"It's my father. His spies must've told him where we are, and now he's trying to ruin everything and get me to leave." I rejected the call and tucked the phone back into my pocket. "Like I said, he never wants me to have fun. But if Bruno went to a game, my father wouldn't say a thing to him."

"Have you ever tried talking to him about it? Maybe

he doesn't see what he's doing. Maybe he doesn't realize he's favoring your brother so much."

I snorted.

If only that were true.

I looked into Natalia's compassionate eyes, her hand still in mine, and I wondered if I should tell her something I'd never told anyone.

"He knows what he's doing," I said. "He's always known. When I was a boy, I was fascinated by guns. Everyone around me had them, so I naturally wanted one too. I asked my father to teach me how to shoot, but he refused because Bruno still didn't want to pick up a gun, no matter what my father tried. After a lot of begging, I convinced Sebastiano to teach me. It was one of the happiest moments of my life. But my father found out."

I looked away from her for a moment.

"I thought he'd be proud of me, and I wanted to show him what I learned. But he grabbed me by the arm, dragged me to my room, and hit me with the back of his gun. When I fell to the floor, I heard him take off his belt. After he was done beating me, he warned me not to ever do anything without his permission again. Then he locked me in and let me out two days later. He almost fired Sebastiano too but settled for taking a month's worth of his paycheck."

"I'm so sorry. That's horrible." Natalia lifted her hand to her mouth, her eyes filled with shock.

I probably shouldn't have told her.

This was supposed to cheer her up, not depress her.

But it felt good. It felt good to tell someone, and I didn't know why. I wasn't looking for compassion or pity.

"After that, my father tried everything he could so my brother would be better than me. Once, he had us take a math test to see who's better at it. Except, he gave us the same test. Bruno already learned all of that at our private school and even had a tutor, but I'd never even seen most of that stuff because Bruno and I obviously weren't in the same grade. When I complained to my father that the test wasn't fair, he punished me for it. For a while, he kept bragging about Bruno's amazing math skills, and he'd always give me this look of disappointment..."

Natalia ran her fingers over mine.

"Bruno and I also had to earn our right to have a birthday party. You can guess who had the biggest parties ever and who never had one because he wasn't good enough. I got very close to having one, though." The corners of my lips tilted up. "My grades were excellent, and I was doing everything right. The only thing that was missing was an essay I had to write and ace, so my father buried me in tasks and missions that had to be done. I had to get up early to get everything done, and when I got home, I was too tired to even think. Refusing to do any of the tasks would give my father an excuse to punish me, so I couldn't do that.

"I managed to write the essay, but I got a B, so no party for me. When my brother got an F, he still got a party because my father said our enemy must've gotten into the school's system and sabotaged the tests. That was one of the most ridiculous excuses I've ever heard, but by then, I already knew Bruno was his favorite and I was never supposed to outshine him. Sometimes I wonder why he hasn't just killed me if he hates me so much."

"Maybe he doesn't hate you," Natalia said.

"He did almost let me die once, but I don't think it was on purpose. Our house caught fire, and he panically went searching for Bruno with Bruno's guard. They got Bruno out, and Sebastiano got me. I was young, but I still remember the surprised look on his face when he saw me, as if he'd completely forgotten I existed.

"He won't try to kill me because he doesn't want to break our code either, and I guess he also wants me to fuck up so badly that everyone will see he's been right all along, but I won't let him win. It will be satisfying to see the look on his face when he loses everyone's support because of his precious son and has to hand the leadership over to me. It's the only reason why I put up with all this shit." I gritted my teeth.

"What if you weren't born into a mafia family? What if you were someone else? What do you think you'd be doing?"

"I don't know. I haven't thought about it. I don't see the point. I am who I am, and there's no way to change that. There's no life for me outside all of this, no matter how fucked up it is, but I'm sure you already know that."

My phone buzzed again.

I wanted to ignore it, but I took a look at the screen again.

It was Sebastiano. I'd left him at home because I had other guards and didn't need him, and he wasn't as strong and as fast as he'd been when he was younger.

Besides, after protecting me my whole life, he more than deserved a break. It was a surprise he hadn't retired already.

"What's up?" I knew he wouldn't be calling without a good reason.

"One of your stash houses was just attacked a few minutes ago."

"Where? Which one?"

"I'll send you the details."

"Okay." I ended the call and turned to Natalia. "We have to go."

The game was almost over anyway.

"What happened?" she asked as we got to our feet.

"An attack." I glanced at my phone. "Shit! I need to take you home first, and by then, it might be too—"

"You don't have to take me home. I'll come with you. I can stay in the car."

"Are you sure?"

She nodded.

Potentially putting my wife's life at risk again was a terrible idea.

I could send her with one of my guards, but I didn't know what had happened. She might be in danger. I didn't want to let her out of my sight.

"Okay. Come."

WHEN WE REACHED THE stash house, it was already too late.

My men stood around the bodies scattered on the ground.

"Stay here," I said to Natalia and got out of the car.

"What happened?" I asked.

"We think it was the Vinicellis, sir."

"The Vinicellis?"

"Yeah. Four cars showed up out of nowhere. Not the ones they usually drive, so we didn't spot them until it was too late. They got out of their cars and opened fire. Five of ours are dead. We got three of theirs."

I went closer to the bodies, inspecting them carefully. "What makes you think it was the Vinicellis? I don't see any of their symbols or tattoos."

"Who else would it be, sir? They're close enough to our territory."

I picked up a discarded gun off the ground, eyeing it carefully.

Once I held the remaining bullets in my hand, I ground my teeth together.

This wasn't the Vinicellis' doing.

It had to be Bruno's.

Or maybe even my father's.

Why would this happen exactly after I rejected my father's call? Why would the Vinicellis randomly attack without any of their symbols?

Random, nondescript cars made sense because they needed to enter our territory without attracting attention, but not anything else.

Why attack and take nothing? It clearly wasn't their intention to steal from me, and if they wanted to make a point, that wouldn't work if they were hiding who they were.

Something was off.

"I know who's behind this. It's not the Vinicellis. Not their jackets, not their guns," I said. "I want you to gather a team. A special team. No tattoos. No symbols. Nothing that could lead to us."

"Yes, sir. What's our target?"

"Bruno's stash house. I'll text you the address." One good thing about being a Cavallaro was that I knew about all of my family's stash houses, which included those that were now my brother's.

"But, sir—"

"He did this, and you answer to me. Do it and make sure no one finds out. Do you understand?" I gave him a hard look.

"Yes, sir."

I could tell he wasn't happy about it. We weren't supposed to be attacking each other, but Bruno had started this.

Not me.

He'd wanted to provoke me and had me rushing at the Vinicellis for revenge. He wanted me to make a mistake, but I wasn't going to fall for his trick.

And I was going to respond in kind. I trusted my men here, and they trusted me. They were going to obey me, no matter what.

Maybe there wasn't enough of them for an open war against my brother and my father, but I could answer my brother's attack.

My father might still find out, but he wouldn't be able to do anything about it because then he'd have to admit what Bruno had done.

If Bruno thought he could defeat me easily, he was wrong.

I'd find a way to defeat him, once and for all.

Tension grew in my body, and I wished I could punch something, preferably my brother's face.

CHAPTER 17

Natalia

AFTER EVERYTHING GIANLUCA had told me, it was impossible not to feel for him. I had no idea what I would've done in his place.

Sure, my sister always seemed to fit in better with the way of life that my family required of us, but our birthday parties had always been the same—or however we'd liked them—and our parents had celebrated our successes equally.

I couldn't even imagine everything Gianluca had gone through.

When he got in the car, his jaw was set. I'd caught a glimpse of the bodies through the window, so I knew some of his men must have died and he was upset about it.

But when he started the car, without even a glance at me, I didn't know what to think.

Maybe he just needed some time to process what had happened or to think about some strategy to get revenge on whoever had attacked his stash house.

Once I realized we weren't going in the direction of our house and the guards weren't following us, worry gripped my insides.

"Do we have to go to a safe house?" I asked.

"No."

"Then where are we going?"

"You'll see."

I didn't like the cold tone of his voice or the empty look on his face.

He stopped the car in front of a small store and got out. I waited for him in the car. When he returned, he had a bottle of whiskey in his hand.

He opened the bottle and took a swig, then offered the bottle to me.

"No, I don't want to drink. Can we just talk about whatever is bothering you? Maybe it will help." It seemed to have helped earlier today.

Even when he'd been telling me about all those terrible things his father had done, he'd appeared more relaxed somehow. His eyes hadn't seemed so dark.

Sure, it was nighttime, and there was very little light here, but I could see the storm in his eyes.

But he was locked away from me.

Blocking me out.

Refusing to let me in.

He placed the bottle in the holder and gunned the engine.

"I want to go home," I said. "It's getting late."

He didn't say anything, just turned on the radio and upped the volume.

I glared at him, hoping that would catch his attention, but he ignored me.

When he finally pulled over, we were in the middle of nowhere. Everything was so damn dark, and there wasn't even any moonlight.

He got out of the car and took the bottle with him.

I waited for a few moments, and then I got out too.

The sounds of waves crashing against the cliffs made me gasp. I hadn't realized we'd gone so far and reached the ocean.

"Gianluca, let's go home. Please."

He took a few more large gulps and then threw the bottle. It smashed into pieces against a rock.

I hugged myself, shivering in the cold wind.

Gianluca pulled his shirt over his head.

"What are you doing?" I asked.

He didn't answer as he kicked off his shoes and took off his pants.

"Gianluca!" I yelled when he broke into a run, straight to the edge of the cliff we were on.

And then he jumped.

My heart skipped a beat, my insides constricting.

I hurried to the edge of the cliff, but it was too dark to see anything.

Was he dead?

I saw a path that led down to the beach that was close by and ran as fast as I could.

"Gianluca!" I screamed.

When I reached the beach, I was out of breath. I looked right and left.

Then I saw him.

He was swimming toward the beach, and when he got out, there was a huge grin on his face.

"What the fuck is wrong with you?" I yelled.

"Do you want to feel free? Really free?" he asked, running a hand through his wet hair. "Then come jump with me."

When he reached out for me, I backed away from him.

He'd clearly done this before, and he knew exactly where the best jumping spot was so he wouldn't get himself killed. But still, it was dark and he'd been drinking.

One mistake, and he could've died.

"You're out of your mind," I said.

"Why are you always so afraid to let go? You can go right back to being a mafia princess when you're done."

"This has nothing to do with letting go, you idiot!"

"Ah, well. You're yelling at me. That's a start." He grinned.

"I'll be in the car." I spun on my heel and strode away from him.

I'd been wrong.

There was no hope for him.

Sure, he could be nice and I did feel sorry for him because of his family situation, but that didn't mean I could overlook his crazy outbursts.

The man who'd shared his past with me might be a good father to my children.

But the boy who thought jumping off a cliff in the middle of the night while drunk because he was upset about something was no father material.

The last thing I wanted was to keep waiting for the moment he was going to change to his other self, as if someone had flipped a switch, and pray that I wouldn't end up hurt or dead because of it.

I wasn't ready to be a mother either, so apparently he and I were a perfect match set up for failure.

I didn't know what to do about that. Maybe I could talk to my dad, and he could get my mom and my brothers away from here safely before my marriage exploded into our faces.

Hopefully, Gianluca would be distracted with Bruno, and he wouldn't have the time to think about me too.

I should've already done something somehow. I could've talked to my mom while Gianluca was away. She could've given my dad a message for me.

I supposed I'd gotten comfortable with Gianluca.

A little too comfortable.

I'd thought that maybe he was different. More open-minded, especially because he hadn't laughed at my dreams like everyone else.

More human.

And he was.

But it wasn't enough.

Tears filled the corners of my eyes.

Gianluca kept calling my name, but I didn't stop.

CHAPTER 18

Gianluca

I WASN'T IN THE LEAST surprised when my father summoned me for a meeting the next day. The attack on my brother's stash house had gone just as planned, and my brother's men hadn't seen it coming.

My father and Bruno were already sitting at the table

when I got there. My father's face was serious, and Bruno was glaring at me.

"Why the grim faces? Did someone die?" I should keep my mouth shut, but I didn't want to. "Or did someone *not* die?"

"Do you think the attacks on your and your brother's stash houses are funny?" my father asked.

"No, not at all." I took a seat. "I wish we knew who'd done it."

I met my brother's gaze.

"It's odd that no one claimed the attacks, even though they were successful," my father said through his teeth, his gaze narrowing at me. "What did you do?"

"Me? Why don't you ask Bruno that?"

"I didn't do anything," Bruno said.

"Neither did I." If he was going to lie, I would do it too.

"Your stash house was attacked first," my father said. "You should've done better at identifying and catching our enemy before they got to your brother. If they know where our stash houses are, then we have a problem."

"If you think everything's always my fault, then why don't you let me really branch out on my own? I'll take what's mine, and I'll protect and take care of it as best as I can. Then what I do won't matter to Bruno and you. I'll operate under a different name, and everyone will know that what I do has nothing to do with you."

"Absolutely not," my father said. "That would weaken the family. Neither of you has heirs." He looked at Bruno. "But..."

I was sure whatever my father was going to say would only benefit Bruno. Maybe he was going to let Bruno get independent with some lame excuse about him being older and whatnot.

"I've made a decision that concerns both of you," my father said. "I'm done waiting for you to do the right thing. Whichever one of you gives me a grandson first gets everything."

"What?" Bruno gaped at him. "That's not fair!"

"Yes, it is. I'm the boss and I decide who will take my place. People like the Vinicellis dared to screw with us because they see the discord and uncertainty over the future leadership in our family. It's time to end that. Our family legacy has to continue, no matter what. Imagine if something happened to the two of you. Without an heir, our men wouldn't have a reason to fight. We would cease to exist and someone else would take over. Is that what you want?"

"No, Father," Bruno said. "But we can't just find an heir in a store and buy him!"

"No, you can't. Your brother is at least married and has a wife. What do you have? Where's your wife?"

Bruno pressed his lips into an angry line.

I kept my face expressionless, but I was laughing on the inside.

Finally, my father was done with Bruno and his bullshit. My brother was in trouble, but this wasn't over yet.

Natalia wasn't pregnant, and I didn't have an heir yet.

But judging by the look on my brother's face, he hadn't seen this coming or planned on it. His fake attack and my retaliation had sent our father in the direction he hadn't been hoping for.

Good.

Once Natalia gave me a son, my brother would have zero excuses.

I was looking forward to that moment.

"I don't think this is a good idea," Bruno said. "I'm the firstborn. In our family, it's always been the firstborn who—"

"And all the firstborns had sons before they turned twenty-five and were married even before that. You had plenty of chances. You could've gotten married," my father said. "But you didn't. I have some families in mind if you want to correct your error. You better act fast because your brother has an advantage now."

Bruno bared his teeth, getting to his feet and almost toppling his chair. He shot me a glare before storming off.

I still had no idea why he was so against getting married, unless he'd been stupid enough to fall for some girl who was never going to be acceptable enough to be the mother of his heir.

My spies hadn't seen him with anyone, but he was good at hiding, so that didn't mean anything.

"Are you really going to go through with this if I have a son first?" I met my father's gaze. "Or are you just doing this to light a fire under Bruno's ass?"

"Yes, I'll go through with it." He didn't even blink. "But don't think you've already won. Not every man sires a son. Some never succeed."

If my father didn't have special requirements, I wouldn't mind having an heiress. I'd seen female leaders in the mafia before, and my family's views felt outdated.

But if I told my father that, he would laugh in my face and told me I was crazy.

"Are we done here, Father?" Things were finally looking up, and even though I was tempted to blow it all up just because I wasn't used to having luck on my side —at least for now—I knew I shouldn't do that.

"Yes, you may go." There was something in my father's eyes when he looked at me, but it was gone so fast that I couldn't figure out what it was.

I got to my feet and strode out of there.

Once I got home, I immediately went to Natalia's

room. It wasn't too late yet, and I felt like celebrating my little win.

And what was a better celebration than a good fuck, especially when I needed an heir as quickly as possible?

It seemed like a win-win.

"Natalia?" I said as I opened the door.

She was lying in bed, her back to me.

She didn't turn around.

Was she already asleep or was she still mad at me because of what I'd done yesterday?

I sighed.

Why had I had to fuck up things with her?

She was the one who could give me exactly what I needed, and for once, I didn't feel so lonely when she was with me.

She was like a ray of sunshine in the darkest, coldest night, but now she didn't want to share her warmth with me.

I closed the door.

We'd talk tomorrow.

CHAPTER 19

Natalia

I LAY ON THE BED AND stared at the ceiling. The dawn was almost here, and I'd been unable to sleep.

One part of me missed Gianluca's touch, and the other was wondering what the hell I was going to do now, because there was no way I could just keep avoiding my husband without putting my family at risk.

When I thought about Gianluca's and my future, I didn't know what to think. Maybe he'd succeed once and get himself killed, but I didn't want that to happen.

A shot rang out, cutting through the silence.

I gasped as I sat up, my heart racing.

Were we under attack?

I hopped to my feet and quickly grabbed a shirt and a pair of pants so I wouldn't be in my nightgown if the attackers came.

The next thing I heard were voices, but no more shots.

The door swung open.

"Are you okay?" Gianluca asked, a gun in his hand.

"Yeah. What's going on?"

"I don't know, but I need to get you to the panic room now. Come." He waved me over. "Stay behind me."

"Okay."

He pulled out another gun he had strapped in the holster around his waist and offered it to me.

"I don't know how to shoot," I whispered.

His eyebrows lifted. "But you're a mafia princess."

"Exactly!"

"Fuck." He tucked the gun back. "Just stay very, very close to me and keep your eyes peeled."

He caught my hand, and I followed him out into the hallway.

While we were on our way to the other end of the house, shouts could be heard outside.

Then someone's loud cry reached my ears.

Eve? It sounded like her.

Gianluca shoved me behind him, shielding me with his body, and pointed his gun at someone who was coming from around the corner.

My pulse sped up.

"It's you," Gianluca said when the guards came into view and lowered his gun, but only a little. "What's going on?"

"An accident," one of them said. "A maid was shot."

"Eve?" I asked.

"No idea. Don't know her name."

"Where is she?" Gianluca asked.

"Last room down the hallway."

Gianluca and I broke into a run. Once we reached the room the man had mentioned, I immediately spotted Eve on the floor, her hand caked in blood covering her side.

The guards who were in the room were holding another guard by his arms. His face was pale, his eyes full of panic.

"Eve," Gianluca said as he crouched next to her. "What happened?"

"I'm dying," Eve cried, as I knelt next to her too.

"No, you're not going to die," Gianluca said, moving

her hand and inspecting the wound. "Did someone call our doctor?"

"Yes, sir," one of the men said. "He's on his way."

"Good. Bring me a towel! Now!" Gianluca's gaze landed on the guard who was being held by others. "And get him out of here."

"No, please." Eve sobbed. "I'm scared."

"There's nothing to be afraid of. You'll be fine. I know it hurts, but you're not going to die." Gianluca snatched the towel someone had brought and pressed it against Eve's wound. "Doc will be here soon. Focus on telling me what happened, okay?"

I got hold of her hand because I didn't know what else to do, but Gianluca seemed to be doing great at distracting her and transmitting her the confidence that she needed.

"It was my fault," she said softly. "I... I... I was secretly meeting with Cole. It was dark, and I didn't realize he was holding his gun. He got startled, and he fired. I'm so sorry. I know relationships aren't allowed among the staff and I would've told you, but..."

Her gaze shifted to mine.

My throat constricted.

She was going to tell him about what I'd done.

Now that her secret was out, there was no reason for her to keep mine.

"It's okay," Gianluca said. "The only thing that matters now is that you get better."

"Cole..."

"Bring him back," Gianluca said to one of his men. "Bring Cole back here."

Eve looked at me again, but her lips were pressed together.

She wasn't going to reveal my secret.

Oh hell.

My shoulders relaxed slightly.

I had to get out of the way because Cole rushed to her as soon as they let him in. He was by her side in an instant, caressing her cheek.

"Thank you," he said to Gianluca, who only nodded.

The doctor and his team finally showed up, and they surrounded Eve in an instant.

"We have to take her to the clinic," the doctor said.

"All right," Gianluca said, getting to his feet. "Cole, you may go with her, but make sure you don't get in the doc's way."

"Yes, sir," Cole said.

As they all put Eve on a gurney, I couldn't look away from Gianluca. His hands were bloody because he'd been holding them over Eve's wound.

Someone else wouldn't have done any of that. Someone else wouldn't give a damn about his maid and wouldn't even care if the maid and the guard were together.

Gianluca had to know Eve would feel better if Cole was with her. Not having him by her side might only upset her and cause her to worry, and she didn't need any of that right now.

Gianluca had done the right thing, and I wondered if maybe, without the toxic influence of his family, he could be a completely different man.

But how could I keep him away from them? How could I show him that proving his father wrong and besting his brother wasn't the only thing in this life that truly mattered, and that it was actually hurting him even more?

I wish I knew the answer to that.

CHAPTER 20

Gianluca

"THIS IS EXACTLY WHY we don't allow relationships," Sebastiano said as he and I watched Eve and Cole from the terrace.

Eve had spent a few days at the clinic, but now she was fine, and she couldn't stay away from Cole.

"If something happens," Sebastiano added, "he'll think about her first and try to save her, not you."

"I don't need saving."

Sebastiano gave me a long look.

"I know what I'm going to do about them," I said. "We have a new safe house that needs to be inconspicuous. The two of them can take care of it while they pretend they're a regular couple living there."

"I don't think that's a good idea."

I watched Eve as she pressed herself close to Cole, who wound his arm tightly around her. They looked at each other and smiled, and then Cole brought his lips down to hers.

There was just something about them. It was as if they were living in a different world, free from any expectations or constraints.

Before, I'd think they were disgusting and shouldn't be acting like this where someone could see them.

But now...

I thought about Natalia. For a second, I wondered if we could be like that, and that maybe it would be nice.

But that was a crazy thought.

"I didn't ask for your opinion. Just get it done," I said to Sebastiano.

There was something I had to do with Natalia, and I didn't want to waste any time.

"QUICKER," I SAID AS Natalia struggled with her gun.

Anyone connected in any way to the mafia should know how to shoot and defend themselves, especially a mafia princess. It didn't make any sense that no one had taught her.

Sure, most of the time, there'd be someone with her to protect her, but that one time when no one was around or if she was the only one left standing, she needed to have a chance at getting away and saving herself.

And Natalia was brave enough to try.

When I'd offered to teach her, she'd happily accepted. She wasn't like some other women—my mother, to be exact—who scowled at the idea and would rather die waiting to get saved than learn a very useful skill.

"I'm trying." She furrowed her brow until she finally got it right.

"Okay, now shoot."

She lifted her arm and aimed. When she pulled the trigger, she flinched.

The bullet missed the target, and her frown deepened.

"I'm terrible at this."

"No one's perfect on their first try, trust me. You're doing just fine." I stopped behind her and guided her arm. "Hold it like this." My fingers brushed hers.

She leaned into me.

Fuck.

When she was so close, it was easy to forget what we were doing. Her scent of roses and something unique to her filled my nostrils, and the way she pressed against me send my blood rushing to all the wrong places.

She pulled the trigger, unflinching this time, and she managed to hit the edge of the target.

"You're getting better," I said, my lips grazing her ear.

She shuddered, her breath hitching. "What happened with Eve and Cole? Did you fire them?"

"No, I sent them to watch a safe house. If the house is empty for too long, people might get suspicious or someone might try to get in. If they think a young couple moved in, no one will think anything's wrong. No one knows Cole and Eve are working for me."

"Really?" She turned around, her eyes filled with surprise and amazement.

"Yeah. It was the best thing to do."

"Does that mean you believe in love now?" She cocked her head.

"I guess some people are lucky enough to find it. But they're not like us."

Her smile faded. "But would you like that? If you were someone else. A regular guy."

I stared deep into her eyes. "I don't know. Maybe. And you?"

"Yeah, I'd love to have a successful career and have someone by my side to share all the good and bad moments with. A family. And we'd be safe and free."

And I want that with you, Natalia.

But I couldn't tell her that.

She was never going to believe me, and it would be stupid to even think we could ever be a regular couple.

"Do you think they'll be happy? Cole and Eve?" she asked.

"I don't know. If they're lucky."

She pressed herself closer to me, her big eyes staring at me as if she could see right through me.

I couldn't resist.

I lowered my lips to hers. Her mouth responded to mine, and I wound my arms around her.

"You should take the gun," she breathed.

"Yeah. Good idea." We didn't need any more accidental shootings.

My fingers brushed hers as I took the gun and placed it onto a table where all the other weapons and things were.

"What did it feel like? To fire a gun?" I asked as Natalia stalked toward me.

Her eyes were sparkling with desire, and even though she usually held back, she seemed much freer now.

"Powerful," she said.

"We'll do it again tomorrow. And again. Until that gun becomes so familiar to you, you can hit the target with your eyes closed."

She bit down on her lip, looking at me through her eyelashes. "Okay."

My cock twitched.

When she reached me, she placed her hands on my chest, pushing me back, and I let her. Our mouths collided again, and she guided me inside.

Her fingers found the zipper of my pants.

When she freed my cock and stroked me, I groaned.

Her thumb circled my tip, driving me crazy, as she pushed her lips against mine.

Then she lowered herself to her knees right in front of me, her eyes focused on me.

My cock throbbed as she took me into her mouth, swirling her tongue over my length.

"Fuck." I grunted as I buried my hand in her hair while she sucked me. "Natalia..."

There was something nagging at the back of my

mind. Something I was supposed to do that I'd forgotten, but it didn't matter now.

I rocked my hips, shoving myself deeper into Natalia's hot mouth.

My mafia princess.

My wife.

Mine.

She was mine, and no one was ever going to take her away from me.

CHAPTER 21

Natalia

I WANTED GIANLUCA TO stay with me. Before we'd gotten here, I'd overheard him mentioning his brother's name, and I so didn't want him to switch back to his dark self.

What he'd done for Eve and Cole was amazing, and when he'd talked about them, I'd seen a longing in his eyes.

A longing he probably didn't even want to admit to himself that he had.

But I'd seen Eve and Cole together.

I'd seen the love in their eyes, and I believed.

I believed they'd be happy.

I believed that love did exist after all. We just had to find it. It wouldn't fall from the sky, though. We had to work for it.

And I was willing to try with Gianluca, especially because of the explosive energy between us.

I loved the look on his face as I traced my tongue over his thick length.

I loved that I could bring him so much pleasure with such a simple touch.

He pulled out of my mouth with a sigh, and then he lifted me to my feet and hauled me up into his arms.

I let out a yelp as I wrapped myself tightly around him. He lowered me onto a sofa, his hands ripping at my clothes.

He kissed me hard, his tongue pushing past my lips, as he tugged my pants and underwear down.

I was already brimming with heat as his fingers parted my folds and rubbed against me. My shirt tore, and he wrenched my bra down.

His mouth instantly closed around my nipple while he pinched the other. A gasp escaped me as he sucked and licked, and a jolt of pain as his teeth grazed me quickly turned into pleasure.

He moved down my body, going straight for my center. His fingers dug into my thighs as he shoved my legs wide open.

His tongue slipped into my slickness, and I arched my back as his every lick brought me closer and closer to my release.

He kept teasing and toying with me, and when I couldn't take it anymore, I let out a loud cry, my body overcome with ecstasy.

Gianluca pulled me up as he sat on the other end of the sofa. His strong arms were around me as he positioned me over his cock.

I trailed my fingers down his chest, and then I cupped him, guiding him inside me. A groan escaped me as I slowly lowered myself down on him, taking him all in.

He grunted as I started rocking my hips, riding him faster and harder while he held me close.

I threw my head back as more heat spread through my body.

And then I met Gianluca's gaze.

I stared into the blue depths of his eyes.

He was there.

The man I liked was in there, and I didn't want him to disappear.

I wrapped my arms around his neck as I slammed myself down on him again and again.

Our releases hit us at the same time, and we both cried out, clinging to each other as if nothing else in the world mattered.

And maybe it didn't.

My lips brushed against his, and then he placed a gentle kiss on my neck.

Once I pulled away from him, trying to catch my breath on the other end of the sofa, I wondered if he was going to leave again.

Sure, this wasn't his or my room, but we were alone, and there was no need to rush anywhere.

I just wanted him with me for a while longer.

Gianluca extended his arm toward me, and I let him pull me into his warm embrace, my head resting on his chest.

A small smile spread across my lips as I lazily traced my finger over his skin.

A buzz of a phone threatened to ruin my bliss, but Gianluca didn't even move to check it.

I pressed myself closer to him.

IT HADN'T BEEN EASY to let Gianluca go, but I couldn't keep him with me forever, no matter how much I wanted to do that and how much I wanted to just take all the time for us to figure out if there could be something more between us.

But as I strolled through the hallways on the way to my room, something else bothered me. Eve was gone, and I was going to be out of pills very quickly.

Yeah, I might have changed my mind about Gianluca, but I was nowhere near ready to have a child with him. Our relationship was still developing and we were still figuring things out. Me getting pregnant could ruin everything and hinder the progress we'd made.

What if Gianluca only used our child to get what he wanted? What if it drew out the darkest side of him?

I found myself going to Eve's old room instead. After making sure no one was around to see me, I pushed the door open and entered the room.

It was now even emptier than it had been, but some of the clothes had been left behind, maybe for the maid who was going to replace her.

I opened the drawer with clothes, and when I picked up a shirt, I found six more boxes of pills.

A gasp escaped my throat. Eve must've brought them here when she'd had a chance because she'd expected I'd be back for more, and she hadn't wanted anything to jeopardize her relationship with Cole.

It was a surprise she'd left it all here when she could've taken the boxes with her, but maybe she'd just forgotten.

I grabbed one of the shirts and wrapped the boxes in it, and then I hurried to my room.

If Gianluca found out, he'd kill me.

Once I got to my room, I grabbed my phone and dialed my sister's number.

I wasn't expecting anything, but the staff actually put me through.

"Hey, Nat. What's up?" Adelina asked.

"When you were pregnant, did you think—"

"Oh, my god! Are you?"

"No, I'm not. I'm just—"

"You have a feeling you are? Then I'm sure you are! I had a similar feeling, but I thought I was crazy. Then I did the test and—"

"No, it's not that. How did you know you were ready?"

"What do you mean ready?" Confusion filled her voice.

"Well, weren't you scared?"

"Why would I be scared?"

I inwardly groaned. Yep, I supposed I was the crazy one here and again making drama out of nothing.

"Are you worried about your husband?" she asked.

"Yeah, I guess."

"Don't be. I know he expects a son, but we're not robots. He'll understand if it's a girl."

I made a face. That so wasn't what I'd wanted to talk about. "I mean, did your pregnancy affect your relationship with Enrico?"

"Oh, a little. He was super pleased with me when he found out."

"What if you'd told him that you needed more time? That you weren't ready to be a mom?"

"Why on earth would I tell him that? That doesn't make any sense."

Right.

"Look, Nat. No one's ever completely ready for anything, but we do our best and learn along the way. You have Mom and me. You're not alone, okay?"

"Yeah, I know. Thanks," I said softly.

"I have to go. Carlo needs me."

"Okay. Bye."

"Bye! I love you!" Adelina ended the call.

I was about to place my phone on the nightstand when it buzzed.

It was a text from Gianluca.

He wanted me to get dressed because we were going out.

Out? Where? What should I wear?

I texted back.

Whatever you want. Something you'd wear on a date.

My eyebrows shot up. A date?

Wow. That sounded fun.

A smile spread across my lips.

Maybe I could forget all my worries for a while and just see what happened, and yeah, I intended to keep taking my pills.

At least for now.

CHAPTER 22

Gianluca

WHEN I WAS WITH NATALIA, days passed very quickly.

And turned into weeks, which turned into months.

I'd been taking her to restaurants so she could try out new food. We'd gone to bars, despite Sebastiano's protests because I'd wanted Natalia to have some fun.

We'd gone swimming and to more basketball games.

We'd even played a game ourselves. I'd taken her to see car racing.

I'd taught her how to shoot, and then showed her some self-defense moves, which usually ended with us having sex. I'd even gone shopping with her because being away from her was unthinkable. Fucking her in the changing room was even more fun.

"Gianluca," Sebastiano called. "I need to speak with you. It's urgent."

"Can't it wait?" I was supposed to watch a movie with Natalia.

"No, I'm afraid it can't."

I groaned. "What is it?"

"It's Bruno. Our spies spotted him with a woman."

"And?" I didn't see the urgency in that.

"She was visibly pregnant."

"What?" I frowned. "Who is she?"

"That's the problem. We don't know. She's not in any database, and our spies lost them before they could get any closer to find out or take a better photo of her face."

"Then find out who she is!"

"I have a team already working on it, but things aren't looking good."

"Who do you think she is? My father won't accept just any child. Bruno knows that."

"Your father might change his mind if the baby is a

boy and your brother's. Unless Natalia is pregnant, and you forgot to tell me."

I swore under my breath. "She's not."

"The woman also might be a relative or a long-lost daughter of some mafia boss from a different area. Bruno might be waiting for the right moment to make his move and convince your father to let him marry her."

"You must find out who she is."

"And you might want to go with Natalia for a checkup, just in case there's a reason why she hasn't gotten pregnant yet."

"Keep me informed. I want to know Bruno's every move."

"I will."

I strode to the room where Natalia was waiting for me. She had a bowl of popcorn in her hands, and when she smiled at me, it was as if the whole room was suddenly more illuminated.

But her smile faded when she saw the look on my face.

"Is something wrong?" she asked.

I usually wouldn't say anything or want to bother her with any of it, but now it felt natural to want to share with her everything that was happening.

In a way, this affected her too.

"Yeah," I said as I settled on the pillows next to her,

winding my arm around her. "Bruno was spotted with a pregnant woman."

"What? Who is she?"

"No one knows yet, but this could change everything. My father clearly said that the one who gives him a grandson first gets everything, but he also wants to make sure that our blood remains pure."

She furrowed her brow.

"Yeah, it sounds absolutely stupid, but my father believes that if you don't marry and have a child with a person who's also from an acceptable mafia family, then the child is worth less. Since my brother refused to marry, everything was perfectly set up for me to finally get everything I've ever wanted. But now... You're still not pregnant and—"

She flinched.

"I know it's not your fault. I don't blame you," I added, just in case she was worried about that. "But if my brother gets a son soon, my father might accept him, pure blood or not. And we don't even know yet who the woman is. She might be exactly what Bruno needs, and he's been hiding her for some other reason. Maybe he's had to negotiate with her father, or there was something else going on that no one figured out. Bruno is good at sneaking around."

"Can't you just put a tracker or a bug on Bruno and find out what he's up to?"

"Doing that wouldn't be easy. We know most of each other's moves. We've been trained the same way. He can recognize my spies, so it won't be easy."

She chewed on her lower lip, her brow creased with worry.

I almost regretted telling her any of it. We should be enjoying the movie, not thinking about my brother.

But some things were inevitable.

I'd be damned if I let my brother win just like that. There had to be something I could do.

CHAPTER 23

Natalia

I WATCHED THE TURMOIL in Gianluca's eyes, and I didn't know what to do to make him feel better. If he knew I was the one who was in his way of getting everything he'd ever wanted...

I wanted to tell him, but maybe now wasn't the right time. These past few months had been wonderful, and we'd been acting like a regular couple so much I'd almost forgotten who we were.

But now it was time to get back to reality. Maybe Bruno was only trying to upset Gianluca so he'd make a mistake. Maybe that woman wasn't anyone important.

But how could we find that out?

This was all my fault. If I was already pregnant, we wouldn't even have to be worrying about this. Or maybe we would, considering Franco's crazy list of requests.

"Is there some nightclub that Bruno loves to go to?" I asked.

Gianluca and I had been to a few, and it had been amazing just to let go and dance until our feet hurt, even if we had to be surrounded by guards in the VIP area.

But it had been so easy to pretend Gianluca and I were alone.

"Yeah. Why?" he asked.

"Well, there's a lot of noise and flashing lights. Maybe someone could slip a bug on him while he's having fun."

"He has his guards, only uses the club's special exit, and he never leaves the VIP area. If he's hanging out with someone, those people have to be checked by his guards first. Slipping a bug on him there would be almost impossible."

"Can you follow him after he leaves the club then?"

"Already tried that, but the club is on a busy street, and it's very easy for him to disappear in the crowd.

Someone can watch from across the street, but then they'd be spotted."

"What about a restaurant? Does he have a favorite restaurant?"

Gianluca nodded. "But you need a reservation to get in, and they won't accept just anyone, so a spy probably wouldn't be able to get in there."

"Could you get in?"

"Yes, of course, but Bruno would recognize me right away."

"What if we go together? What if you talk to him and distract him, and I figure out a way to slip a bug on him?"

"Absolutely not. I'm not letting you go anywhere near him after what he did to you." His face darkened.

"Right. But what if we get a table farther away from him? And then I go to the bathroom to disguise myself, and when I walk past him, he won't know it's me." I was willing to do just about anything, no matter how crazy it sounded, because I really wanted the whole thing with Bruno to be a ruse. "Maybe I can pretend to be a random girl who's interested in him. He might fall for it."

I didn't want to be the reason for Gianluca's failure.

Then stop taking the pills. That would be a start.

I pushed that thought away.

"No," he said, placing his hand on my cheek. "You're

mine. I won't let him even look at you, and I refuse to put you at risk like that."

He kissed me then, his lips pushing against mine with a bruising force.

My lips tingled when he let me go.

He caught my arm, tugging me to him and pulling me over his lap. His hand rested on my ass, sending a shot of heat through me.

"You'd want to seduce my brother, huh?" He caught the waistband of my pants and underwear and yanked them down, exposing me to him.

"It was just a thought," I said, barely able to stifle a moan as he ran his hand over my bottom.

He brought his hand hard on my ass, making me yelp, but the sting only added to my arousal.

"It wouldn't work," he said, and unleashed a flurry of smacks all over my cheeks.

I let out a gasp, wishing he'd move his fingers to my wetness. As I spread my legs wider, he gave my pussy a light slap.

I wanted to rub myself against his hand, but he held me tightly in place and kept driving me crazy.

"Do you know why it wouldn't work?" he asked, shoving two of his fingers inside me.

"Please," I whispered. "I want you... inside..."

"You didn't answer my question." He pulled me up, his lips colliding with mine with so much hunger that I thought he wanted to devour me.

"I don't know," I whispered.

He pushed me down, making me gasp. I was on my stomach, wishing I could rub myself against something to relieve the pressure inside me.

I heard Gianluca take off his pants.

He shoved my legs apart, and then he rammed himself inside me. His body enveloped mine as he forcefully pushed in and out of me, making my moans louder and louder.

My insides throbbed and tingled as his hips slammed against mine.

"He'd know..." Gianluca said into my ear as he dove even deeper inside me. "Because you'd smell like me."

I cried out as my orgasm shook my whole body with so much force that I felt as if I were floating.

Gianluca's lips brushed my shoulder, and then he sank his teeth into my skin.

I let out a groan, every inch of me pulsating with pleasure.

"You belong to me," he breathed into my ear. "Only to me."

As he spilled himself inside me with a grunt, he held me tightly, not letting go.

I didn't want him to stop touching me either, because when his skin touched mine, I felt safe.

I felt powerful.

I felt comfortable.

Instead of rolling off me, he pulled me with him so I ended up in his embrace, resting on his chest.

As I tried to catch my breath, I suddenly had another idea.

"It's your birthday soon," I said.

"Yeah." He didn't sound too thrilled about it.

"Why don't we throw you a party? For your family."

"What?"

I shifted so I could look into his eyes. "Think about it. You said your father never wanted to throw you a birthday party. Have you thrown a party for yourself?"

"No." A frown creased his forehead. "I didn't see the point. I'm not a kid anymore."

"Well, you can do it now. You can invite your whole family, including Bruno."

"Why would I do that?"

"So you can maybe talk to him, or you can slip a bug on him. He wouldn't have his guards, and he doesn't know his way around our house. We can throw the party at some other place if you want. But it might be our best shot."

"It'll be suspicious. He won't come."

"It won't be suspicious. You have me. I can be the one who wants to throw you a party. If your father comes, your brother will too. Bruno won't want to miss it. He can't know if you're planning to use the opportunity to announce something else, or he might think you could get closer with your father. Even if he doesn't show up, I think it's worth a try."

"That might not be a bad idea. If I could get my hands on Bruno's phone, I could put a bug and a tracker in it."

"Great. I'll take care of everything so you don't have to worry about it."

"Thanks." He pressed his lips against mine. "But if Bruno goes anywhere near you or tries anything, I'm kicking him out."

"Sure." I gave him a small smile.

But Bruno would be stupid to try something in our house, right? I had no idea why he'd attacked me, and he'd never said anything to Gianluca either.

I just hoped I could avoid him and that Gianluca would do what needed to be done.

And then, maybe I'd feel a little less guilty about my secret.

CHAPTER 24

Gianluca

I'D LEARNED A LONG time ago to ignore my birthdays. Sebastiano was the only person who'd wanted me to celebrate, but I'd ordered him to stop trying, and he respected my wishes.

Even though Natalia was throwing me a party today, I knew it was only so I could try to get a bug on Bruno and find out what he was up to.

Nothing would be different this year.

The mouthwatering smell of food made me open my eyes. Natalia had fallen asleep in my bed last night. I'd held her in my arms.

But now she wasn't next to me when I reached out for her. I rolled over and sat up.

"Happy birthday," Natalia said with a smile on her face. "I made this for you."

She was wearing a sexy red nightgown, and I could barely force my eyes away from her thighs.

She placed a tray with food on the bed.

"And I got you something." She bit down on her lip, and my gaze fell on the bags on the floor.

For a moment, I was speechless.

"I hope you like—" She didn't get to finish the sentence because I caught her hand and pulled her on the bed with me. "Wait! We're going to knock the tray off—"

"Who cares? I'm starving. Starving for you." I tugged her closer, burying my face between her breasts. "You're the only present I need."

She let out a laugh, which was like music to my ears.

This was already the best birthday ever.

I looked up into her eyes, and I wanted to tell her something.

Three words I'd never said to anyone.

"I invited my family, and my sister and her husband to the party. I hope that's okay," she said.

"Yeah, sure." I kissed her.

Kissed her like I'd never kissed her before, and my only birthday wish was that she'd never leave my side.

"DO YOU LIKE IT?" NATALIA asked.

I looked around our back yard. "Wow."

Not even my brother's parties had been this big. The table was huge and the chairs were dark blue.

There were plenty of flowers around, but they'd been tastefully arranged. Nothing too much, but not too little either.

"There are five different versions of your cake," she said. "So if you have a preference, you can pick one."

"Actually, I want all five out."

"Okay." She grinned. "I picked the menu myself, and I think there'll be something for everyone. Oh, and Sebastiano told me to invite some of your relatives too, so I did."

"Perfect." I planted a kiss on her lips.

"Hey! Don't do that! You're going to smear my makeup!" she said, her face serious, but her tone told me she was joking.

"You look amazing. Have I told you that already?" I looked her up and down.

She was wearing a beautiful black cocktail dress with silver sequins that revealed her legs. It wasn't going to be easy to stay focused on the party when she was close to me.

"Yeah, you told me like five times already," she said.

"And I'll keep doing it."

"Looks like the first guests are here."

"Yeah. Let's go greet them." I offered her my arm, and she took it.

Then we headed toward my relatives.

After we were done with them, I spotted my father and headed to him while Natalia was still busy talking to one of my aunts.

"Father," I said. "I'm glad you could make it."

"What is all this?" he asked, narrowing his eyes at me. "Is there something you want to share with me?"

"It's my birthday, in case you forgot." I flashed him a smile. "Is that not enough?"

My father stared at me, his face deadly serious.

"Welcome, Mr. Cavallaro," Natalia said with the

sweetest smile ever. "Please allow me to show you to your seat."

My father's gaze met mine, and then he followed Natalia.

My brother strode toward me, looking around as if he thought this was a trap and someone was going to jump out at him.

"Bruno," I said.

"Gianluca. I didn't expect you'd invite me here."

"Maybe I wanted you to see what a real birthday party with family looks like. But if you don't want to be here, you can leave."

"I don't believe you. You're twenty-six, not sixteen. What are you up to, huh?" Bruno took a step closer.

I glared at him. "Stay, and maybe you'll find out."

I walked away from him.

"Everything okay?" Natalia asked.

"Yeah." I snaked my arm around her waist, keeping her close.

"I think I know how you can get his phone." She leaned in to whisper into my ear. "I'll distract him. His phone has to be in his jacket, right? He'll have to take it off. How quickly can you open his phone and get that bug or whatever it is inside?"

"A couple of minutes," I said. "But I already told you. You're not going anywhere near him."

"I'm going to be fine. Please trust me. He's not going to do anything with so many people around."

"We thought the same at my father's dinner."

"I'm not afraid of him. You'll be close by. Nothing will happen."

I gazed into her eyes.

She was so certain about this.

I trusted her, but I didn't trust Bruno.

"I'll go get my purse first, okay?" she said. "My gun's in it. If Bruno tries anything, I'll shoot him."

The corners of my lips tilted up. "Okay."

Gone was the innocent girl who was afraid of her every move.

"Your parents are here," I said.

She followed my gaze, a smile breaking out on her face. "Come!"

She grabbed my hand, and I let her pull me with her.

I felt someone's gaze on us, and I looked directly into Bruno's eyes. He was watching us with suspicion, a serious look on his face.

Good.

Let him stare and wonder what the hell I was doing.

If things worked out, I might finally find out who the hell the pregnant woman who'd been seen with him was.

And then, I'd do anything to fuck up his plans.

CHAPTER 25

natalia

LUCKILY, MY PURSE WAS black and had a thin strap, so I didn't have to worry someone was going to see it and wonder why the hell I had it with me. I could always say I needed my makeup with me because we were eating.

But distracting Bruno was impossible.

He was looking at everyone like a hawk. And yeah,

his phone was in his suit jacket. I'd seen him pull it out once to take a look at something. But it didn't look like he was going to take off the jacket, even if it was quite warm here.

I met Gianluca's gaze. We had to do something, or Bruno was going to leave.

I had an idea.

Picking up my glass of wine, I strode in the direction of the house. Just as I reached Bruno's chair, I pretended to trip.

I caught myself on the table right next to him, and just when he turned toward me, I tipped my glass. The wine spilled all over the front of his white dress shirt.

"Oh, I'm so sorry," I said as Bruno got to his feet, looking at his ruined shirt. "Please come with me to the bathroom. I'm sure there's something for stains there that can help. If we wash it out quickly, it should be as good as new."

"Is your husband going to let you?"

"Um, it'll be fine. It won't take long. And he's busy right now." I glanced at Gianluca, who was talking to his relatives, but I was sure he'd seen what I'd done.

If I left with Bruno, he'd follow, and that was all we needed.

"Fine." Bruno got to his feet, and he and I strode to the house.

"The guest bathroom is over here," I said as I led him

down the hallway. "In here." I opened the door for him. "Oh, can I take your jacket? It'll be easier to—"

"Yeah." He shrugged out of his jacket, and then he unbuttoned and took off his shirt.

I hung the jacket on the door handle, from the outside, and then pulled the door closed just enough so that Bruno wouldn't see Gianluca.

I hoped like hell this would work. Bruno was already trying to wash his shirt in the sink.

"There should be something in here." I opened the cabinet, looking for some soap.

"It's fine," Bruno said.

"I'm really, really sorry," I said. "I can go get you one of Gianluca's shirts if you want."

"No." Bruno was still washing his shirt, but he turned to me, his gaze traveling my body. I reached for my purse, wondering what the hell he was looking at.

My hands?

My neck?

My stomach?

I noticed the door moving slightly in the mirror, and I knew I had to keep Bruno's gaze away from it.

"Do you forgive me for my mistake?" I ran my hand over my neck, lifting my hair.

Bruno's eyes followed my movements.

"Don't worry about it. It doesn't matter."

"I hope I didn't ruin the party for you. Did you like the cake?"

"It was great."

I kept smiling at him, unsure what else to do.

"Natalia! Are you there?" Gianluca called from somewhere down the hallway.

"You should go," Bruno said.

"Yeah, sure." I gave him another small smile and then I hurried out.

Bruno stayed in the bathroom, but one of the guards was now in the hallway, so there was no risk he'd try to go somewhere else.

We would still need to have the house and the yard checked, just in case Bruno—or another one of Gianluca's relatives—had also come up with the idea to leave a bug somewhere.

"Did you do it?" I whispered to Gianluca.

His lips spread into a wide smile as he took my hand. "Come. It's time for my speech."

Gianluca led me to the spotlight with him.

Bruno showed up a few moments later.

I averted my gaze and instead focused on my sister, who was smiling at me.

"But first, I need to mention someone special," Gianluca said, tugging me closer to him. "My wife. Without her, none of this would've looked as good as it does."

"We know!" someone shouted.

"Without Natalia, my life wouldn't be the same," Gianluca said, his eyes on me.

Everyone started clapping, except for Gianluca's father and Bruno.

My sister was clapping too, but her smile had faded.

What was that look in her eyes?

Envy?

Was that even possible or was I imagining it?

But then I remembered she'd organized a party for Enrico too, and he'd spent the whole night bragging about his achievements. I didn't think he'd even mentioned her once. She'd been sitting at a different table, with other women.

Forgotten.

And I was right here with Gianluca in the spotlight.

Adelina had no clue what Gianluca and I had pulled off with Bruno. Would Enrico ever even trust her with something like that?

I didn't think so.

When I was a child, I'd thought I had to be like her. I'd thought I had to adhere to my family's rules and be perfect to have a chance at a good and happy life.

But none of that seemed to matter.

The only thing that mattered was the person you were spending your life with.

And Gianluca was nothing like Enrico.

WHEN THE PARTY WAS over and everyone was gone, I took a seat in one of the chairs. The party had been a success, and I assumed Gianluca was already checking if the bug was working.

"Hey," he said softly, placing his hands on my shoulders and massaging gently.

"Is it working?"

"We'll see. I just wanted to thank you again. Best birthday ever."

I placed my hand over his and craned my neck so I could give him a smile. "Glad to hear it."

He leaned forward and pressed his lips against mine. "We should go inside," he said. "I want this day to last a little longer."

"Okay." I let him pull me to my feet, and then we headed to the house, his arm around me.

CHAPTER 26

Gianluca

"I HAVE A VERY IMPORTANT task for you," I said to Sebastiano as soon as I spotted him.

"What do you need?"

"I put a bug inside Bruno's phone. If he hasn't found it, you know what you have to do."

"How did you manage to do that?" Surprise filled his eyes.

"I had help from my wife."

A smile spread across his lips.

"What? Why are you smiling like that?"

"No reason."

I raised an eyebrow at him. "Never mind. Just listen for any clues as to what Bruno might be up to. Since we still don't have any news about the mysterious woman, this is our best shot at finding out what his plan is and stopping him."

"If I hear something, should I come find you or text you?"

"Text me. Natalia and I have plans."

"All right." Sebastiano was grinning again.

What the hell was wrong with him today?

"One more thing," I said. "Tell someone to prepare the biggest room in the house for Natalia and me."

Separate rooms no longer made sense since we were always sleeping together, either in her room or in mine. Having one room would make things way easier.

"Of course," Sebastiano said.

I glanced at the time on my phone. It was still early, but maybe Natalia was ready, so I headed straight to her room.

I opened the door.

Natalia let out a gasp, something white falling out of her hand.

A box was in her other hand.

Birth control pills.

I'd trusted her, and she...

She'd betrayed me.

Shock and anger mixed and rushed through me like a wave, erasing everything else.

"What the fuck are you doing?" I raised my voice as I started toward her.

CHAPTER 27

Natalia

I INSTINCTIVELY STEPPED away, my back hitting the wall, the box with pills falling out of my hand.

"Gianluca, I—" I didn't get to finish the sentence because he caught my wrists and trapped me with his body against the wall.

"What the fuck did you do?" He bared his teeth, his face red with anger.

"I'm sorry." I stared deep into his eyes, willing my Gianluca to come back.

Willing him to push past the anger so we could at least talk.

His whole body was rigid, his face contorted.

And even then, I wasn't afraid of him.

"Gianluca," I said softly, but I didn't think he could hear me, so I did the only thing I knew that might make things better.

I lifted my head and brushed my lips against his.

He closed his eyes with a sigh, his mouth responding to mine. Heat spread through me in an instant, and I knew he could feel it too.

"I want to punish you," he whispered, rubbing his erection against me through our clothes.

"Then do it." I bit down on my lip, letting out a soft moan as his grip on my wrists intensified.

His mouth was on mine, ravaging and hungry. I was breathless as he yanked me to him and tugged at my dress.

The zipper broke, and my dress fell down my body as his lips landed on my neck. I groaned as his hands roughly kneaded my breasts and then ripped the clasp of my bra.

He kept kissing me, his hands going down my

stomach and into my wet panties. A moan escaped my lips when he pushed me on the bed so I ended up on my hands and knees.

He tore at my panties, leaving me naked and exposed and so aroused that I could barely think.

I heard him pull his belt out of the loops.

The belt swished through the air, landing on my ass with a loud smack. I jumped a little at the unexpectedly intense sting.

My center throbbed with need as the blows kept falling one after the other, setting my bottom on fire.

Gianluca brought the belt down hard on my sit spot, making me cry out.

He ran his fingers over my sore cheeks before giving me a few hard smacks with his hand.

"Please," I whispered, wishing him inside me.

He let go of me, and I heard him move behind my back, his clothes rustling as he took them off.

I was like a big bubble of need waiting to burst.

Gianluca climbed on the bed, capturing my arms and tying them behind my back with the belt. My face rested against the bed, and I moaned into the sheets as he shoved my legs apart.

He parted my folds, and then he rammed himself deep inside me so hard and fast that I gasped.

His fingers wound in my hair, keeping my head

down as he pumped into me, each merciless thrust bringing me closer to the delicious peak.

The world around us seemed to disappear, and all I could focus on were the sensations all over my body as he pounded into me.

When my release hit me, I let out a loud cry, my pleasure exploding through me in waves.

Gianluca pulled out of me and rolled me over. His hand cupped my jaw.

"Open your mouth," he commanded, and I obeyed.

He positioned himself over my mouth, and then he slipped his throbbing cock into my mouth.

I tried to take as much of him as possible. With a groan, he slammed himself all the way to the back of my throat, making me gag.

Then he spilled himself into my mouth.

Once he pushed himself up and lay on the bed next to me, we were both breathless. The taste of him lingered on my tongue, and I wiggled my hands out of the belt, freeing myself. My insides still pulsated with pleasure.

"Why?" he asked softly, staring at the ceiling.

"I'm not ready."

His gaze found mine as he turned his head. "You wouldn't have to do anything. The kid would have a nanny and everything. You wouldn't even have to change any diapers."

"No, that's not it."

He looked away from me. "Right. It's me."

"What?"

"You want a child, but not with me."

"No, I didn't say that."

"Then what is it?" Hurt flashed in his eyes when our gazes locked.

"I'm just not ready. I don't know how to explain it. I want to have children, yes, but not now. We're only just getting to know each other and it's nice. I don't want to... I'm scared everything will go wrong. Hell, I'm still getting to know myself too. I just felt like we'd be having a kid for all the wrong reasons—not that I don't understand them—but it just doesn't feel... safe. And we haven't even talked about what we want for our children... What kind of life they'd have. But I know why you married me, and I know giving you an heir is my duty, so I'll stop taking the pills and—"

"No."

My pulse sped up. He was going to divorce me, and the deal with my family was going to be over, wasn't it? I'd screwed everything up.

"Gianluca, please." I pushed myself up. "Please give me a chance. I didn't mean to hurt you. If you divorce me—"

"Divorce?" He sat up too, his brow furrowing. "Who said anything about that? You're my wife. You're mine."

He reached out for me and pulled me into his

embrace. We fell back on the bed, and I pressed myself tightly to him.

"Maybe you're right," he said. "Having a kid just because we have to have one doesn't feel okay. We'd bring him or her into a huge mess, especially if my brother ended up winning somehow."

"But what about your dream? I know how much you want to be boss." I searched his eyes.

"I'm going to figure something else out."

"Are you sure?"

He nodded. "You're right. We need more time. We can't bring a kid into this life without a plan or without any thought just because it's supposed to be our duty, and just because everyone in our families has been doing it like that for decades. But you have to promise me one thing."

"What is it?"

He placed his hand on my cheek, caressing. "Promise that you won't think less of yourself because of this."

"No, I—"

"I know some part of you still thinks your sister is perfect, even if her life isn't, but you need to let go of that."

I wanted to argue, but I couldn't. "It's not easy to just forget everything I've been taught my whole life."

"I know, but we can start new traditions. New rules. Or no rules." He grinned.

"Okay." My shoulders relaxed.

Maybe he was right. He and I were who we were. Why would we have to be like the others in our families?

This was about our life together, not anyone else's.

It was about our happiness and our choices.

"But you have to promise me something first too," I added.

CHAPTER 28

Gianluca

"PROMISE YOU WHAT?" I asked.

"Promise me that you didn't just agree with me because you're sabotaging yourself."

"What?" I blinked at Natalia.

"Come on, Gianluca. I know what it's like to feel like you're in the shadow of your sibling and that you're never going to get out of it. And your situation is like a thousand times worse than mine. Doesn't a part of you always expect you will fail and your brother will end up the one winning, no matter what you do? Do you subconsciously believe you're never going to beat him? Do you believe you'll prove your father right? Is that why it's easier for you to jump off a cliff than accept you're worthy of happiness and love?"

I stared at her, wanting to laugh about the crazy things she'd just said.

But, deep down, I knew she was on to something.

"When you asked me why I was taking the pills," she said, "what was your first thought?"

"That no one in their right mind would want to have a kid with me."

"Why?"

"Like you said, I can be reckless and self-destructive. The only thing I've ever wanted out of life was to best my brother and prove my father wrong. Now that I think about it, that sounds completely stupid and pointless. My father hates me. Even if he has to give me everything, he'll still hate me, and my brother will hate me even more. I'll get a second of satisfaction. Maybe. And then what? I guess I didn't think I deserved anything more."

"And now?" She tilted her head.

"And now... I see there are other things that matter in life." I pulled her closer to me. "I don't want to be like my father. I don't want to destroy my children's lives and raise them in the same shitty way my father raised me. I don't want to repeat his mistakes, and the mistakes of my ancestors. I didn't want to see it before or even think about it because being different already felt like a failure. But when I really think about my father and my brother, neither of them is happy. I know that. It makes no sense to want to be anything like them."

Natalia smiled, planting a soft kiss on my lips.

"We're going to figure out our own path. Who cares about what anyone else wants or expects of us?" I brushed my lips against hers. "Fuck. Why didn't I think of this earlier? Why did it take me so long? I feel better than I've felt in my whole life. I finally feel free."

"Don't blame yourself. Blame our families. We just didn't know any better. We've been told our whole lives that we were failures if we didn't fit the mold. Maybe not always in those exact words, but we felt it. We saw the disappointed looks, heard the whispers... until we started to believe it was all our fault. And you know why you didn't have any other dreams and goals? Because they stifled any interest we had in anything other than what was expected of us."

"I wanted to play basketball when I was a kid at one point," I said. "But my father thought I was wasting my time, so he had our maid throw away anything basketball related I had. I managed to save one ball."

"The one in your closet?"

He nodded. "How did you know?"

"I was curious about you."

My eyebrows shot up.

"I saw your sketches."

"Another thing my father threw away. Burned most of them, actually. Right in front of me. He said sketching was pointless and not masculine enough."

"Ouch. No wonder your father is so angry all the time at everyone. He must be miserable when he doesn't have any hobbies and never has any fun."

"Probably." I pulled away from her, looking for a piece of paper and a pen.

"What are you doing?"

"I'm going to do a sketch of you."

Her eyes widened. "What? But I'm naked!"

"So what? I love when you're naked." I found what I was looking for.

Natalia lay back on the pillows, a big smile on her face.

She was so fucking beautiful.

I wanted her to be happy, and I wanted to be happy with her.

My phone buzzed, making me groan.

I snatched it, just in case it was something important. Sebastiano's name was on the screen.

"Hello?"

"I have some news," he said.

"What is it?"

"Your plan worked. Bruno talked to that woman. The baby's not his."

A smile tilted up my lips. "Do you think he's going to try to lie about it to my father?"

"I don't know."

"Okay. Thanks for telling me." I ended the call.

"What's going on?" Natalia asked.

"The mysterious pregnant woman... The baby's not Bruno's. There's a chance Bruno will lie to my father about it. Maybe fake a paternity test or something. But if he does that and my father finds out, Bruno is done for. My father loves to play games with people, but he hates when someone tries to play him."

"What are you going to do about it?"

"Nothing for now. I'll wait and see what Bruno does."

Maybe Natalia and I were ready for a different kind of life, but getting free from the mafia, especially my family, wasn't that easy. I'd have to come up with a plan.

"But for now, let's get back to having fun." I picked up the pen and paper again.

"Can I see it?" Natalia asked and laughed.

"Later. When I'm done."

She pouted, and I wanted to kiss her again.

Why had I ever thought I needed in my life something other than her? Everything else could burn down to the ground, but if she was still with me, it wouldn't matter.

CHAPTER 29

Natalia

GIANLUCA'S FATHER HAD called him for a business meeting or something like that—Gianluca wasn't sure either—so I used the opportunity to pay a visit to my family.

Gianluca had made sure everyone knew that I didn't need his permission if I wanted to go somewhere. He only wanted my guards to be with me.

"Something's different about you," my mom said, narrowing her eyes at me. "You're glowing. Are you—"

"No, Mom. I'm not pregnant," I said. "Gianluca and I... Well, we realized we really like each other."

"That's great to hear! But I must say I'm not surprised. I saw the way he was looking at you at that party you threw for him. I'm so happy for you."

"Mom, I have to ask you something." I lowered my voice, even though my brothers were far enough away not to overhear anything, and none of the staff was close by either. "I heard something... about you and some... um, guy."

Her smile faded, sadness filling her eyes.

"So it's true?" I asked.

She nodded. "It was a long time ago. I felt trapped in my marriage. Unhappy. Then I met him. When I was secretly meeting with him, I felt free, and it was all very exciting. But it was doomed from the start. Your father inevitably found out, and he and I reached an agreement. He made me choose, and I decided my family was more important to me than some passing affair."

"I'm so sorry."

"Don't be." She waved her hand. "Just don't mention it to anyone. It's all in the past."

"Sure." I glanced at the time on my phone. "I should go."

"Your husband already wants you back?"

"No. There's something I need to do. Gianluca and I are moving into a bigger room and I wanted to find some things to decorate."

"That sounds nice."

"Yeah."

"All right then, honey."

We got to our feet, and I gave her a big hug.

"You leaving?" Ciro asked as he and Gabriel came running toward us.

"Yeah. Come here."

They both embraced me.

I lifted my gaze.

My dad waved at me from the terrace, and I waved back.

Once I reached my car, one of the guards opened the door for me.

While we were on our way, I browsed through some websites on my phone.

Suddenly, the tires screeched and the car lurched to a stop. A gasp escaped me when I realized our car was surrounded by four SUVs.

"Get down," one of the guards yelled as he pulled out his gun and jumped out of the car.

I lowered myself down, searching for my gun in my purse, my pulse in overdrive. The guards opened fire, and I could hear the bullets as they hit our car. The glass was bulletproof, but I didn't know if that would be enough.

One of the guards screamed, and I risked a peek in his direction. Our attackers—all masked in black—opened the door and were dragging the guard out.

I had to get out of here.

I opened the door and slipped through it. As I crouched next to the car, I lifted my gun. When I spotted one of the masked men coming toward me, I fired at him.

He went down.

I looked around.

If I could get to the alley across the street, then maybe I could get away and disappear.

My breath caught in my chest when my other guard stumbled back not too far away from my hiding spot. He went down, blood pooling under him.

I slowly pushed myself up as the gunfire ceased. The attackers were shouting.

One of them jumped out in front of me, and I shot him.

Then I broke into a run, pushing my feet as fast as they'd go.

I didn't hear any more shots.

Whoever it was, maybe they didn't want me dead.

Just as I was about to reach the alley, something hit me in the shoulder.

It wasn't a bullet.

I glanced at my shoulder as the ground started to dance in front of my eyes.

What the hell was that?

Dark spots appeared in my vision, and I had to catch myself on the wall to stop myself from falling.

My body was suddenly heavy, my vision blurry.

Someone was coming my way, and I pointed my gun at them, but I couldn't focus.

The gun clattered out of my hand.

I collapsed to the ground.

And then the world went dark in front of my eyes.

CHAPTER 30

Gianluca

MY PHONE RANG JUST as I was on my way home. My father had finally wanted to discuss a strategy for defeating the Vinicellis with me, and I assumed it was because Bruno had failed to do it once again and only made them angrier.

Since they were closer to my territory, I knew I had to do something about them before they got bold and made a move against me, and if my father agreed to give me some of his men too, then I was all for it.

"Yeah?" I said as I answered.

"Gianluca!" Sebastiano said, his voice full of panic.

I'd never heard him so distraught.

"Your wife's car was attacked. The guards are all dead. She's gone. We don't know where she is."

Hearing those words was worse than having a knife cut straight through my chest.

"How the fuck did that happen? Where was she?" I asked. "I'm on my way. Everyone should be looking for her. Everyone. Search the traffic camera footage."

"She was on her way to a store. I can text you where we found the car, but there aren't any cameras in that area. The attack must've been carefully planned."

I swore under my breath, my heart racing.

I would find her.

I had to.

"ANYTHING?" I ASKED as soon as I burst into the house.

Sebastiano was on his phone, a worried look on his face. "No. But everyone's looking for her. She couldn't have disappeared."

"Do you think they'll kill her?" I hated the hint of desperation in my voice.

"If they wanted to do that, we would've found her body with the others. The Vinicellis have been spotted crossing into our territory, but we don't know if it's related."

"Fuck!" I raked my hand through my hair. "I need to go to the spot where the car was found. Maybe there's something everyone missed. A clue of some kind."

"We'll find her," Sebastiano said.

I paced up and down.

My phone buzzed.

I checked the screen.

Bruno.

What the hell did he want?

"What?" I snapped. "Now's not a good time."

"Why? You missing something?"

I froze, clutching the phone tightly in my hand. "What the fuck did you just say?"

"I have your wife."

"You son of a bitch! If you dare to even—"

"Calm down, brother. She's fine. For now."

"What do you want?"

"First, you're not going to tell Father about this. Second, if you want her back alive and in one piece, you'll come for her to the address I'll send you. You'll come alone and unarmed."

"Are you out of your fucking—"

The line went dead.

I gritted my teeth, my fingers curling into fists.

"He has her," I said. "Bruno has her."

"What?" Sebastiano's eyes widened in shock. "What does he want? How dare he—"

"He wants me. He wants me to come alone and unarmed."

"You can't do that." Sebastiano crossed the distance between us in a few quick strides, his eyes hard on mine. "I know what you're thinking, but if you do what he says, he'll kill you."

"And if I send a team to get her, he'll kill her!" I shouted.

"Gianluca, you need to calm down." He reached out for me, but I stepped away from him.

"I can't fucking calm down. I love her, okay? I love her! I don't want to live without her!"

"Call your father. He'll talk to Bruno."

"Bruno said he'd kill Natalia if I did that."

"Then we'll figure out something. I know you care about her, but you'll lose her anyway if Bruno kills you."

"I know, but she'll be alive. You will take care of her and keep her safe from Bruno and anyone else. You'll make sure she has everything she needs."

"Gianluca—"

"No, it's my decision. I'm going." I headed to the door.

"Gianluca!"

I didn't stop.

My phone buzzed.

I had a text with the address. When I took a look at the map and found a photo of the house, I realized Bruno had planned this very carefully.

The house was in the middle of nowhere, and it had a wall fence. Easy to defend. Easy to see who was coming.

Easy to kill Natalia if I made a wrong move.

Sebastiano ran out after me. "We should talk."

"There's nothing more to talk about. But you'll have to be close by. Far enough away so that Bruno doesn't kill Natalia because of it. Once she gets out, you'll have to come for her and get her to safety."

"What if Bruno doesn't honor your deal?"

"He will."

"How are you so sure?"

"He's my brother." Despite everything, I was sure Bruno wouldn't go back on his word.

I'd still have to be careful, of course.

I couldn't afford to make a mistake.

I couldn't fail.

Not now.

Not with this.

Getting Natalia to safety was the only thing that mattered.

CHAPTER 31

Natalia

WHEN I OPENED MY EYES, I was lying on the floor on a blanket. My head hurt, and I groaned.

Once I pushed myself up, I realized I was in a cell of some kind, or a very big cage.

I gripped the bars, trying to get out, and then I spotted Bruno sitting in a chair outside my prison.

"Let me out of here!" I yelled.

"Calm down. Everything's going to be all right. I'm going to save you," Bruno said.

Save me?

What the hell was he talking about?

He was just sitting there, and it didn't look like he was going to release me.

"Then what are you waiting for? Get me out of here!" I said.

"I'm afraid I can't. Not until he comes."

"Who?"

"Your husband."

"What?" I gaped at him. "Please don't do this. I don't know what you want, but this isn't the way."

"I'm not going to hurt you. All I want is Gianluca. He might not give a damn about you, but he'll come here because of his pride. Once I have him, I'll let you go."

"What are you talking about? What are you going to do to him?"

"Kill him. You'll be free after that."

"No! You can't do that! He's your brother!"

"I know it may not seem like it, but you'll be fine without him. You know that. Then you won't have to hide your bruises and—"

"What bruises?"

"That turtleneck dress with long sleeves? I've met

some mafia women who wore those often, and I know what they were hiding."

"Excuse me? That's ridiculous. I liked that dress. And I wasn't hiding anything. Why would you even think that? You were the one who attacked me!"

"I'm sorry. I only wanted to see how bad it was."

"Are you on something? Because this doesn't make any sense. You believed Gianluca was abusing me, so you thought it was a great idea to grab a potentially scared, vulnerable woman and expose her bruises? Wow, congratulations! You're an idiot!"

"I said I was sorry. I was angry, and it might have clouded my judgment. I wanted to confront Gianluca, but my father got in the way—"

"Gianluca didn't hurt me. You don't need to save me from him. Can you let me go now?" Well, Gianluca might have hurt me a little, but I'd enjoyed every second of it and craved more.

I wasn't going to share any of that with Bruno. He was obviously crazy.

"You don't understand. He's a monster," Bruno said. "He's always been like that. If you don't give him a son soon, he'll kill you. If he hasn't hurt you yet, it's only because of that."

"You're wrong about him."

"When he was a boy, he only learned how to shoot so he could kill my dog."

"I don't believe you."

"Then he killed the girl that I liked at our school."

I shook my head. "That's not true."

"He pretended none of it had happened too. He's good at that. He lies and manipulates, and everyone believes he's a good guy."

"No."

"Do you think he'd die for you? If he comes here, it'll be just so he can save his honor. He'll pretend he's done everything in his power to save you, but he'll let you die to save himself."

"I don't want him to die for me! He's your brother. I know you have some issues, but can't you just talk it out?"

"You'll thank me one day. It's fear talking now, but once you're free, you'll learn that there's so much more in this world to enjoy."

"Bruno—" I didn't get to finish the sentence because a large screen behind Bruno's back that had been turned off suddenly came to life.

It was a camera feed.

Gianluca stood next to a tree, eyeing the camera.

My heart thudded loudly in my chest.

He was here, wasn't he? He was outside wherever this place was.

No!

"Brother," Bruno said. "I'm glad you're here. Now come inside, and I'll let your wife go."

"No! Gianluca, don't!" I screamed at the top of my lungs.

"Give me your word. Give me your word that you'll let her leave the house free and unharmed."

"You have my word. I'm not a monster like you."

"All right. I'm coming." Gianluca lifted his hands up.

"No!" I shouted.

"See you soon, brother."

The screen went black.

"Can't you see?" I said to Bruno. "You were wrong. He's coming. Please end this and let us both go. Your father won't forgive you for this. You will break your family's code. No one will want you as their leader after they find out what you did."

"I don't care about that, and we'll see how far Gianluca is really willing to go for you."

"Bruno, please! Don't do this! Don't fucking do this!" I looked around my cell, but I couldn't see anything that I could use as a weapon or to free myself.

No, no, no!

A few moments later, I rushed to the other end of the cell because I could see a door opening.

Gianluca entered, his hands up. Masked, armed men were behind him.

Bruno had his gun out too.

"Come closer," Bruno said.

Gianluca glanced at me. "Everything's going to be okay."

"Gianluca, no!" I cried.

"Get in here." Bruno opened the door of another cell, and Gianluca walked inside.

"You have me now. Let her go as you promised."

"I will. But you need to do one more thing first." Bruno held up something in his hand and then kicked it under the door of Gianluca's cell before I could see what it was. "Slit your wrists."

"What? No!" I grabbed the bars again. "Gianluca, don't! Please!"

"It's okay, Natalia. You'll be fine," Gianluca said.

I pressed my face against the bars, tears streaming down my cheeks.

Gianluca made a long cut along his wrist, then the other. "Happy now, brother?"

Bruno stared at him with surprise in his eyes.

"Now let my wife go," Gianluca said as his blood dripped onto the floor.

Bruno started toward me, a gun in his hand. It was aimed at me, so I backed away. He unlocked the cell.

"Get out," he said. "My guards will escort you out."

"No! I'm not leaving Gianluca!" I glared at him.

"Natalia, please," Gianluca said. "Just go."

"No, I don't want to!"

"Go, or I'll shoot you," Bruno said.

I took a deep breath, wondering if Bruno was going to shoot me anyway, and then I stepped out of the cell. Bruno's guards were waiting for me, and they grabbed me by the arms.

As they dragged me away, I thrashed and screamed, but it was of no use.

"Gianluca!" I shouted so loud that I felt like the whole house shook.

Why had he done that?

How could I save him?

What could I do when there were so many guards in here?

Every step that I had to take was leading me farther and farther away from him, and it was like agony.

If Gianluca died, how was I going to live without him?

And I hadn't even told him that I loved him.

Tears streamed down my face.

Everything was lost.

CHAPTER 32

Gianluca

I SAT DOWN ON THE FLOOR, watching my blood pooling in the cracks in the stone.

"Show me," I said. "Show me that she's safe."

"As you wish." Bruno turned on the big screen.

I watched the guards as they led Natalia out of the house.

She was crying. Sebastiano approached, wrapping his

arms around her and trying to drag her away from the house.

Safe.

She'd be safe.

That was the only thing that mattered.

"Promise me you won't go after her or Sebastiano. She'll need someone by her side," I said.

"I don't care about him or about her," Bruno said, getting to his feet and stepping closer. "I didn't think you'd do that."

"What? This?" I lifted my bloody wrist. "It's a small price to pay."

"Your life is a small price to pay?" His eyebrows arched.

"Yes. You'll understand if you ever fall in love."

"Love? You love her?" He gaped at me.

"No, I gave my life for someone I hate." I rolled my eyes at him. "Come on. Even you are not that dense."

"You've always said you didn't believe in love."

"Natalia changed my mind."

"I wish you'd changed your mind earlier. But after everything you've done, you don't deserve to be happy with her."

"Maybe, but who are you to decide that?" I met his gaze.

"You've always done everything to make my life miserable."

I let out a laugh. "Me? Your life? Are you fucking kidding me? Kill me, but don't fucking pretend I'm at fault here."

"You killed Archie. You killed Sara."

"What? Archie? Your dog? He ran away."

"Yeah, the lie Father told me because he was covering for you, but I found the body. I know it was you. Your gun was buried with him."

"Father took my gun and never gave it back. He was furious with me because I learned how to shoot before you did. Is that why you tried to drown me?"

"Yes, and you're lying."

"Why would I lie now? What do I get out of it? You're going to let me die anyway."

"And Sara? You were the only one who knew how much I liked her. Her body was full of bruises." His eyes were glassy. "She was only sixteen. What the fuck did you do to her, huh? If Father hadn't sent you away after that, I would've killed you."

I furrowed my brow, leaning my head against the bars. "Fuck."

"What? You admit it?"

"No. I told him. I told Father." I pressed my head harder against the bars. "He was going on and on about your perfect grades, and how perfect everything you did was, and I got angry... I told him you had a secret girlfriend. I'm sorry. I was only thirteen. I didn't think about what he might do."

"Don't try to blame everything on Father."

"Ask him then. Ask him and see what he says."

"Maybe I will, but you won't be around to see it."

"I don't give a fuck. He'll be proud of you."

"Why do you say that?"

"For making this look like a suicide. He'll finally be rid of me, without breaking his precious code. He'll have an excuse to give you everything, as he always dreamed, and he'll erase my existence because once again I'll prove to be an embarrassment and a failure."

"What are you talking about? Father loves you."

I snorted. "Remember that basketball game we had to play at school? Your team against my team? Father loved me so much that he came to my room the night before and beat the shit out of me so I wouldn't be better than you. He knew how much I loved basketball, and he took it away from me."

"He told me you decided not to play anymore because I won, and you couldn't handle it."

I laughed. "Nice one."

"You were always trying to compete with me. Anything I tried, you had to try it too. I had to push so hard to even get a chance to impress Father."

"I didn't. He made me. If I didn't do it, I'd get punished. Do you really think I would've taken a math test I'd never even gotten a chance to study for because I believed I could magically do better than you? Yeah, right. Father was always bragging about you to everyone. It was always you. Never me."

Bruno shook his head. "You didn't see him when he and I were alone. He'd say I did a good job, but then he pointed out how you, even though you were younger than me, could do so well, and how I needed to be even better. It was a nightmare. Sometimes, I barely slept and barely ate so I could get all the work done."

"At least he told you, you did something well." I closed my eyes.

I was just so damn tired.

Tired of everything.

"Gianluca?" Bruno's voice was distant.

I felt like I was floating.

Using the last ounces of my energy, I pictured Natalia's face.

I should've told her.

I should've told her that I loved her.

CHAPTER 33

Natalia

"NATALIA, PLEASE! LET'S go," Sebastiano said, trying to pull me away from the gate.

"No! I'm not going anywhere! Gianluca's in there! Bruno is going to kill him!"

"We need to go."

"I know you care about him too. How can you just

leave him in there and not do anything?" I screamed in his face.

"Because it's what he wants. I've always respected his choices, even when I didn't agree with them."

I burst into tears, letting him pull me into an embrace. As I sobbed, I reached for Sebastiano's gun. I pulled the gun out of his holster.

"Natalia!"

I strode away from him, hiding the gun behind my back, and hurried to the guard who was watching the gate.

Before Sebastiano could stop me, I aimed the gun at the guard's face.

The guard was so surprised he didn't even have any time to react.

"Let me in!" I said. "Or I will blow your face off!"

"Natalia!" Sebastiano yelled.

"Don't touch me, or I'll shoot you too!" I said to him. "I'm getting Gianluca out of here."

I held the gun pointed at the guard's face, but more armed men showed up, and their weapons were trained at me.

Shit.

"Gianluca wouldn't want you to do this," Sebastiano said. "He gave me clear instructions on what—"

"I don't care! I want him!"

The roar of an engine startled me. A few moments

later, a van pulled over in front of the gate. A group of people ran out. They had a gurney with them.

Someone was shouting something to the guards that I couldn't hear, and the guard in front of me touched his earpiece.

"What's going on?" I asked.

"Put the gun down," Sebastiano said.

I followed his gaze.

Bruno was standing at the front door, and I aimed my gun at him, anger coursing through my veins.

But then I saw Gianluca.

They were putting him on the gurney.

His eyes were closed, his face pale.

My heart thudded so loudly in my chest that I thought I was going to faint. I lowered the gun as I realized they were rushing Gianluca to the van.

"Gianluca!" I raced to him.

"Ma'am, please get out of the way," one of the men said.

"I'm his wife!"

"Come with us," a woman said.

Sebastiano was waving his hand, trying to get my attention. He was shouting something, but I didn't care.

I got in the van with Gianluca.

It didn't even matter where we were going, but it looked like all the people in the van were trying to help him. They'd wrapped his wrists.

Were they doctors? Was this an ambulance? But some kind of undercover ambulance since the people were wearing black and there were no symbols of any kind anywhere, but they had all the right equipment.

I sat back, letting them do their job.

"Is he going to be okay?" I asked, but no one answered my question.

I could only hope that I wasn't going to lose him.

I PACED UP AND DOWN the hallway of a small private clinic. Every moment seemed like an eternity, and a part of me wished I'd shot Bruno anyway.

But he was the one who'd called for help. Something must've changed his mind.

I supposed it didn't matter, if Gianluca recovered.

If he died, I was going to put a bullet in Bruno myself.

"Ma'am?"

I spun around to face the doctor.

"You may come in to see him."

Relief flooded me as I rushed into the room.

Gianluca lay on the pillows. Some of the color had returned to his face.

His lips spread into a small smile when he saw me.

"Hey," he said softly. "Am I dead?"

"Luckily, no."

"Prove it."

I leaned forward and pressed my lips against his. "Better?"

"Better."

I caught his hand, caressing his fingers, as I sat on the edge of the bed. "What happened?"

"I don't know. Is Bruno here?"

"No, he's not."

"I want to tell you something."

I gazed deep into his eyes. "What?"

"I love you," he said.

"I love you too."

"I should've told you that earlier."

"Me too." The corners of my lips tilted up.

I kissed him again, and I was happier than I'd ever been.

CHAPTER 34

Gianluca

ONCE I RECOVERED, BRUNO texted me because he wanted to meet with me and talk.

Natalia wasn't so sure if I should go, but since he hadn't let me die when he'd had the chance, I wanted to know what he had to say, even if I didn't know if I could forgive him for putting Natalia at risk.

I made my way to the bar where we were supposed to meet, looking around to make sure this wasn't a trap.

Bruno was sitting at one of the tables, his head bowed.

He looked up at me when I settled in the chair across from him.

"Brother," I said. "I have to say I didn't see this coming."

"Me neither." He sighed. "Look, I'm sorry. I didn't realize... I thought Father was hard on me because I was the firstborn, and that you were trying to sabotage me all the time. But after what you told me, I know now there's a different side to the story."

"Are you saying he screwed us both over?"

He nodded. "Every single thing he did must've been carefully planned. He pitted us against each other. Made sure we were never close enough to talk things through and realize what he was doing."

"We can agree that our father is a sick fuck. What else is new?"

"I'm sorry for what happened with Natalia. I believed you were a monster after what happened to Sara, so I thought Natalia was your victim too. I did some research. Father hired someone to kill Sara and make it look as vile as possible."

"I'm glad we cleared that up."

"I think it's time," he said.

"Time for what?"

"To take what's ours."

I cocked my head at him.

"Father is old, and let's face it, we've been taking care of shit for him for a very long time now. His men are on our side."

"You want to kill him?"

"No. We should go to him and tell him to retire. We'll show him that we know now exactly what he's done to us. We'll take over everything. Divide it between us. And he'll have to watch us both succeed."

A smile curved my lips. "That sounds like a very good plan."

"I know. So are you in?" He offered me his hand.

"I'm in."

We shook hands.

"Who was that woman?" I asked.

"What woman?"

"Pregnant one."

"Someone I saved from her violent husband. He's one of the Vinicellis' men."

My eyebrows shot up. "Really?"

He nodded.

"Then how about, when we take over, we take out the Vinicellis for good?"

"Sounds like a plan, but you'll have to take the lead on that one because you're better at dealing with them."

"I didn't think you'd ever admit that out loud."

He shrugged. "When we're united, they won't stand a chance."

I agreed with that.

There might be hope for my relationship with my brother.

We just had to free ourselves of our father first.

"WHY ARE YOU SMILING like that?" Natalia asked, eyeing me with suspicion.

"Bruno and I went to see our father."

"And?"

"And we convinced him to retire. We divided our territory in two so we can both lead without answering to anyone. We'll defend ourselves from our enemies together, though."

"That's amazing!" Natalia laughed as I wrapped my arms tightly around her.

"You're no longer a mafia princess. You're a mafia queen." I kissed her until we were both breathless. "I have something for you."

"What?"

I pulled out a rolled-up piece of paper from my suit jacket and offered it to her.

She arched an eyebrow at me as she took it.

I watched her eyes widen as she unrolled it.

Her mouth fell open.

"Is this real?" she asked.

"Yeah. If you want to go to college and become a lawyer, this is your chance."

"Is that safe?"

"The college is in our territory, so yes."

She grinned, throwing her arms around me. "How did you manage that?"

"Pulled some strings, but your grades were awesome too, so you earned it."

"Thank you." Her lips collided with mine, and then I couldn't stop kissing her.

She tugged at my suit jacket, sliding it off my shoulders. My cock was already straining against my pants as I pulled her shirt over her head.

Our clothes were gone in an instant, and I loved her soft moans as I kissed my way down her body.

I twirled my tongue around her nipple, my fingers gliding down her stomach and between her legs.

She was dripping wet when I pushed my fingers inside her.

Her body responded to my touch so wonderfully, and when I dove inside her, filling her to the brim, she held onto me.

Her hips lifted to meet mine, and she groaned as I fucked her hard and fast.

"Gianluca," she cried out when I tipped her over the edge, my release joining hers.

My mouth found hers, and I pulled her into my arms, never intending to let her go.

She belonged to me, and I to her.

Forever.

EPILOGUE

Natalia

"LET ME TAKE IT," ADELINA said, catching my bag.

"It's fine. I can manage." I placed my hand over my stomach, rubbing gently.

"You should really stop working. My niece is going to be here soon."

"Oh, come on. Just one more signature, and you'll be

free from that asshole. I just hate that it's taken you years to open your eyes, but I'm glad you finally did. You deserve someone who can really love and appreciate you, and not Enrico."

"I know. Thank you so much for helping me. If I'd gone to anyone else, Enrico would've had them killed."

"You know Gianluca and I will always protect you. And Carlo too." Getting my nephew out of Enrico's clutches hadn't been easy, but Adelina had managed to sneak out of the house with him during the night.

No one had ever expected her to make such a move, especially not Enrico.

"Thanks," she said. "Oh, look who's here!"

I followed her gaze.

Gianluca was waiting for us in front of his car.

A smile spread across my lips, and I waved at him.

"So, I know you're finally ready, but is he?" Adelina asked.

"He is. It's just taken us a few years."

"More than a few."

I rolled my eyes at her as I laughed.

When we reached Gianluca, I wound my arms around his neck and placed a big kiss on his lips.

"I have a surprise for you," he said.

"Oh? What kind?"

"You'll see when we get home."

"Okay." I narrowed my eyes at him.

"DO YOU REALLY HAVE to keep my eyes covered?" I asked as we slowly moved forward because Gianluca was holding his hands over my eyes.

"Almost there."

"It's our home. You can't really surprise me with—"

He moved his hands off my eyes.

A gasp escaped my lips.

The empty room next to ours had been turned into a nursery. Tears filled my eyes as I watched the crib, all the toys, and the drawings of cute animals on the walls.

"Are you okay?" Gianluca asked, a worried look on his face. "If you don't like it—"

"I love it!" I kissed him again. "Did you do those drawings?"

He gave me a nod.

"They're amazing."

"I'm working on a picture book for our princess," he said.

"Aww!"

"You're crying again." He wiped the tears off my face.

"Yes, because I'm happy!"

"I'm happy too." A big smile spread across his lips.

I pressed myself close to him, looking forward to our future.

There was no more fear.

No more feeling like we were never going to be enough.

No more feeling like we didn't belong.

We had each other, and that was the only thing that mattered.

ALSO BY OLIVIA ASHERS

Stuck

Only His

Payment

Not Safe

Indebted Bride

Belonging to Him

His Entertainment

https://oliviaashers.com/books.html

Printed in Great Britain
by Amazon